ALMASI SHEIKHS

The Sheikh's Contract Fiancée

The Sheikh's Unruly Lover

The Sheikh's Pregnant Employee

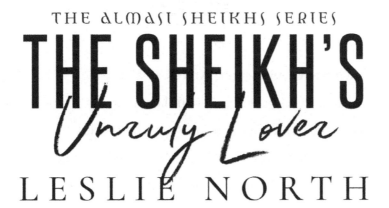

THE ALMASI SHEIKHS SERIES

THE SHEIKH'S
Unruly Lover

LESLIE NORTH

BLURB

Following a recent merger, American executive assistant Marian is sent overseas to meet with her company's new Arab business partner. But once Marian sees who she'll be working with—the handsome Sheikh Omar Almasi—she's instantly wary of his good looks and brooding demeanor. When circumstances force her to step into her boss' shoes, Marian is more than ready to prove she should be taken seriously…even if it means working side by side with the surly, sexy sheikh.

Two years after losing his wife to cancer, Omar is more driven than ever in his family's oil business. He opposed the merger with the US tech firm, and now that it's done, he refuses to compromise himself for corporate Americans. But Omar is caught off guard when he meets beautiful, business-savvy Marian. The woman drives him wild with her stubborn determination and her distracting allure. He's never had to work so closely with someone so…feminine, and the more time they spend together, the more he has to fight his impulses.

Soon their attraction is undeniable, but with the wound of his wife's death still not healed, Omar may never be ready to move on…unless Marian can show him how to love again.

Thank you for purchasing 'The Sheikh's Unruly Lover'
(Almasi Sheikhs Book Two)

Leslie North is the USA Today Bestselling pen name for a critically-acclaimed author of women's contemporary romance and fiction. The anonymity gives her the perfect opportunity to paint with her full artistic palette, especially in the romance and erotic fantasy genres.

Get SIX full-length novellas by USA Today best-selling author Leslie North for FREE! Over 548 pages of best-selling romance with a combined 1091 FIVE STAR REVIEWS!

Sign-up to her mailing list and get your FREE books:
leslienorthbooks.com/sign-up-for-free-books

For all books by Leslie North visit:
Her Website: LeslieNorthBooks.com
Facebook: www.faccbook.com/leslienorthbooks

TABLE OF CONTENTS

CHAPTER ONE

"Marian!" Her boss's voice grumbled through his office and out to her desk by the doorway. She perked up, for maybe the fiftieth time that day, and rose to her feet.

"Yes, Mr. Thomas?" She glided into his office, an eyebrow lifted. He'd been so needy today—exceptionally needy. As his executive assistant, she was used to all the rumbles and rhythms of his routine, but today, all day, she had felt a strange energy in the air. Like an unexpected punctuation mark.

She stood in front of his desk and scanned the piles of papers littering the surface. Ever since the merger with Almasi Holdings, the company in Parsabad, he'd been more of a mess than usual. Secretly, she thought it had something to do with his losing his only daughter—her own best friend—Annabelle to the sexy foreign guy. Or maybe he was just growing senile. He was getting old, after all. And maybe that's part of what she liked about her job. The chance to excel and really keep things together.

"We have some things to talk about." He gestured to the seat facing his desk. "Sit."

She plopped down into the seat, her ruffled skirt lifting slightly as she did. "I didn't see this on our agenda for today."

"It wasn't on our agenda." He barely looked at her as he finished scribbling something down. "I have a proposition for you."

Marian stiffened. This was job talk. She didn't like things that might change her job, which she loved and was perfectly comfortable with. "What is it?"

Mr. Thomas stopped writing and set his pen down, eying her. "Almasi-Thomas needs you in Parsabad."

Marian stared at her boss for a few moments, unsure how to respond. Too many thoughts swirled there, and this proposition seemed so *sudden*. She and Annabelle had been joking for months that sooner or later, her work as executive assistant might take her to Parsabad but…it had been funny. Not an actual possibility.

"Seriously?"

"Our Chief Technology Officer needs an assistant on his upcoming trip," Mr. Thomas said with a sigh. "There's nobody else who can do it but you."

"But—"

"You'll be able to see Annabelle, too. That will be nice."

Marian nodded. "Yes. But I imagined my first visit to her might be more of a vacation. Not a…work trip."

"Does the fact that it's a work trip make it different?"

"No, of course not. It's just…" She glanced at the ground, struggling to find the right words. I just love New York a lot, and change makes me nervous, so maybe you could just not subtly threaten my job with unexpected shifts?

"You know Kelly is a bit…" Mr. Thomas floundered for the word. "Brusque, let's say. I'm worried he won't fare well over there, especially after what Annabelle has told me about the company he'll be negotiating with. So I need you there to keep him in line. Smooth him out. You're good at that."

She sat up straighter, smiling. "Yes, I am."

"So you'll do it."

Marian deflated into the chair again. "Yes, I suppose."

Mr. Thomas grinned a little—an uncommon sight for him. "The flight will be next week. I'll need you to help Kelly finalize a deal with an oil technology company in Parsabad, National Oil. It shouldn't take longer than a week."

He turned to his computer, a subtle way of dismissing her that she knew exactly how to read. She could read this man like a children's book. But the CTO, Kelly? She'd seen him when he'd come through the office to meet with Mr. Thomas and at C-level executive meetings. He'd acted like she was just this side of non-existent. "Brusque" didn't begin to describe him.

So, this is gonna be a fun trip. Marian sidled back to her desk, immediately reaching for her phone to text Annabelle.

"Guess what girl…I'm coming to see you a lot sooner than I expected."

Marian fought a grin. That, at least, was exciting. Only six months apart and it felt like she hadn't seen her best friend in a decade. They were more sisters than friends, and not being able to see her friend daily, especially during Annabelle's new, exciting relationship, made the distance feel immense. Annabelle's response was quick, even though it was almost ten p.m. in Minarak, the capital city of Parsabad.

"My father told me he had some new offer for you. How long will you be in Parsabad?"

Marian tapped out a quick response. "A week. Not bad. Enough time to get into trouble with my girl."

"Plenty of trouble," Annabelle wrote back. "I can show you all around…maybe snag you a Parsian boyfriend before you leave."

Marian giggled as she reread the text. Yeah, a foreign boyfriend. Just what she needed for her life in NYC.

She stuffed the phone back in her desk and got to work, mind on fire with thoughts of what her first international trip in almost five years might end up being like. And if Imaad's brothers were anywhere near as hot as he was…well, maybe a Parsian fling wouldn't be so bad after all.

A week later, Marian touched down in Parsabad for the first time in her life. She eyed the cityscape from the back seat of their car. The city glittered like a jewel in the night sky, all spotlights and steel angles. The road followed a river winding through the city, well-lit promenades along its bank. The city didn't seem asleep so much as ready to party.

She glanced over at Kelly, whom she'd detested within the first three minutes of their trip. Not only did he look down his nose at her, he only listened to her when she prefaced her words with "Sir" or spoke with urgency. Otherwise, he barely acknowledged her existence.

Marian hated feeing small more than anything else in the world. And even though Mr. Thomas had given her a pay bump for this deal-making mission to the Middle East, she couldn't help but feel as if he were punishing her for some reason. Yet another pompous man to handle and tolerate in the business world.

Like there weren't enough of those already.

Kelly was a stinging thorn in her side, a constant irritant who actively stole her joy and fascination at experiencing the new world around her. She had no idea what to expect of Parsabad other than the snippets she'd caught from Annabelle's first six months. But now, with Kelly attached to her hip, she had a growing suspicion she could expect pure kickback and condescension.

When the driver slowed to a stop in front of their five-star hotel, Kelly was out the door before the car had even stopped completely. She hurried after him, eager to mediate should Kelly be an asshole. Given his behavior at the airport check-in counter, the security line, the boarding gate, and ground transportation in Minarak, she could safely assume he had another spectacular quip waiting to fly out of his sorry mouth.

The driver delivered their suitcases a moment later, cheerfully saying something in Farsi that sounded like a happy send-off. His tone said more than his words.

"Is it too much to ask for a driver that respects my time? *And* speaks English?" Kelly muttered it more to himself than to Marian.

Marian sighed. "He's being helpful, *Kelly*." She received her luggage with an overdone smile, as if to make up for the negative vibes from her unpleasant companion.

Kelly snatched his luggage and bolted toward the sliding doors of the hotel, leaving her in his dust. Marian gaped after him, then turned to the driver.

"I'm sorry about him." Marian pressed a bill into his hand. "Please accept my apologies."

Marian strutted into the hotel, distracted by the opulent surroundings. White tile gleamed and stretched around her, the entire west wall of the foyer a gently whooshing waterfall. The wall behind the reception desk, where Kelly stood, boasted rows of live plants. Marian stood behind him, blinking at her surroundings, trying to relish this awe and wonder before he wiped it away again.

As she approached Kelly pocketed his room key.

"Did you check me in too, or…"

"I'm pretty sure you're able to do that on your own," Kelly snapped. "See you at the dinner."

He stomped off, his rolling luggage clacking behind him. Marian set her jaw, taking a breath before addressing the receptionist. She received her key card and headed for the elevators, checking her watch. Only ten minutes until the dinner with the executive from Almasi Holdings. Could that be the bug up Kelly's ass? *Seems like he has more than a bug up there. An entire colony, maybe. Of fire ants.*

Marian's belly rumbled on her way up in the elevator; she was ready for some exciting foreign food. She pushed into the room, taking only a perfunctory glance before scurrying around to freshen up. New shirt, a splash of water on her face, a new layer of deodorant…ready to go. She stepped off the elevator again with one minute to spare and ran into Kelly heading for the restaurant at the same time.

"Did the Almasi rep make the reservation in his name or—" she started.

"I'll be there in a minute," Kelly said, condescension dripping from his words. Marian gritted her teeth, approaching the hostess podium at the hotel restaurant while he veered off elsewhere. *Hopefully to go flush his head in a toilet.*

"Hi, do you have a reservation for Gunther?" She paused. "Or it may be under Almasi?"

The hostess consulted her sheet and then nodded. "Follow me, please." Marian, wedge heels clicking against the wood floor, followed her through the moodily lit restaurant. The hostess led her to a table set for two where a gorgeous man sat alone, flanked by empty tables and turning an empty glass in circles.

The hostess headed straight for him, and Marian slowed, unable to rip her eyes off him. *That can't be our executive.* Her mouth parted slightly as she took him in—dark brows set in a straight line, plump lips, a skin tone that exemplified caramel candies. He wore a dark gray suit with a skinny, trendy tie. He looked up at her just as the hostess gestured his way.

"Enjoy your meal," the hostess said in heavily accented English as she stepped away. The god man stood up, offering a large hand. Marian gaped at it.

"Pleasure to meet you. You must be the CTO that I've heard so much about."

Marian slid her hand into his, a rush of warmth coating her insides. He felt heavenly. Like a glove she'd been looking for her entire life. "Hello. And you are…?" She knew his name—had it in her carefully researched notes a million times—but every thought left her brain at his touch.

"Omar Almasi." He flashed a bright grin, showcasing perfect white teeth, and gestured toward her seat. "Your technology-deal facilitator and unofficial tour guide while you're in Minarak."

A giggle escaped her, completely unsanctioned, as she sank into the plush dining chair. Polished silverware glinted at the edges of an enormous silver plate. A candle flickered between them. This had all the makings of a rom-com date, if only Kelly weren't on his way.

Shit. Kelly. The memory of his existence came to her like a surprise quiz in high school. She swallowed hard, unwilling to relinquish the private time with this handsome stranger.

"Are you Imaad's brother?" She batted her eyes a little, toying with a ringlet by her face. The two place settings screamed at her, but she ignored it. Just for a bit longer.

"I am." Omar's dark eyes glinted like he had a secret. "Do you know him?"

"Not personally, not yet. But Annabelle is my best friend." She said it proudly, as if name-dropping a celebrity. Omar nodded, the corners of his lips turning up.

"So we have Annabelle in common." He shifted in his seat, his tone growing husky. "Very interesting."

Someone cleared their throat, and Marian whipped around to see Kelly looming over her, his crooked nose looking like a sloppy Mr. Potato Head from this angle.

"Were you planning on allowing me to attend my own dinner?" Kelly's voice made her wince.

"Oh, yes. Of course. Sorry, Kelly, I just…" Marian hopped up from the seat, her cheeks burning at the disdain in his voice. And the fact that she had failed to mention she wasn't the CTO. *Damn his distracting good looks.* "I'll ask the hostess to bring you a seat and place setting."

"Good." Kelly eased into the seat she'd vacated, but Omar rose.

"Wait."

CHAPTER TWO

Omar couldn't believe his eyes.

In front of him, the most beautiful woman he'd laid eyes on since his wife's passing two years ago floundered in the face of a type of passive rudeness Omar had never witnessed in his life.

"Here. You take my seat." He gestured for the brunette beauty to take his seat, staring pointedly at the newcomer. Omar had been pegged to meet the CTO of Thomas Petrochemicals, the American division of Almasi-Thomas, so why were two people here? He had barely had time to register the name of the visiting American, much less any supporting details. *Like the fact that this woman looks like someone I need to take home immediately.*

The woman slipped into his seat gratefully, and Omar strode to the hostess stand, explaining the situation in efficient Farsi. He waited by the table as a server brought a chair and arranged the additional place setting.

Once he was settled and glancing between the two recent arrivals, he said, "Okay. Now explain: which of you is Kelly?"

"I am." The balding man with skin the color of pale oatmeal held out his hand. "My name is Kelly Gunther. CTO for Thomas Petrochemicals. I assume you're from the Almasi tribe."

Omar lifted a brow. The woman next to him sighed.

"Correct. And you are…?" He turned to the brunette, loving the way her deep brown eyes went wide.

"I'm Marian Frank." She smoothed the edges of her napkin. "Here to assist Kelly with this deal."

"Great." Omar flashed a wide grin, determined to bring this meeting back to lighthearted territory. His primary function was to help navigate this deal to a successful conclusion. Launched by the American side of their newly merged companies initially, the Minarak office would play a pivotal role in securing the deal; Almasi was a crucial Middle Eastern liaison with the notoriously reluctant-to-negotiate oil technology company, National Oil.

Kelly turned to Marian, his eyebrows forming a hard line. "Go grab me a whiskey, would you?"

Her eyes narrowed to slits. "Do you really think—"

"Allow me." Alarm bells went off in Omar's head—who did this guy think he was?—but he played it cool, signaling for a waitress. "I'll ask the server, not my guest," he added with a pointed look to Kelly.

The flush in Marian's cheek was unbearably cute, though he wished it came from better circumstances. Tension filled the air, and Omar cleared his throat when their waitress finally arrived.

"Please bring us a round of waters, a whiskey for him." He pointed at Kelly. "And anything else they might want."

"I'll take any martini you have," Marian said, sending the waitress a flat look. "Just make it strong."

Omar squashed a grin. How he wished this meet-up could be only the two of them. "Now, let's get back to business."

The three of them—really mostly he and Kelly—chatted about the details of their upcoming itinerary. Tomorrow morning, they'd meet the CEO of the reclusive oil tech company. The three of them would sit in a meeting with the National Oil executives to review their respective proposals. Hopefully all would go well, and a deal could be brokered. They might be looking at a signing by the end of the third day.

"I don't know how they could turn us down," Kelly muttered over his whiskey. "Only a goddamn idiot would reject this deal."

Marian's brows lifted—the silent response system he'd been cataloguing all evening. She seemed familiar to him in a way he could scarcely articulate. She looked nothing like his late wife, Anahita, yet Marian possessed a warmth that reminded him *only* of Anahita.

Omar tried not to think too much of his late wife. Her passing, after only six short months of an arranged marriage, had been too big of a blow. The cancer had moved swiftly, too swiftly for even the best doctors to intervene. And their marriage was now a cracked shell of a memory. Too quick to even document much beyond the wedding. Snippets of their life together haunted him.

But the worst part was not knowing—what would have become of him and Anahita? What children had they missed out on? The love they found together in so short a time was mostly born of grief and rapid bonding…turning a stranger into an intimate lover in mere months.

His heart squeezed in his chest, and he took a sip of his water. Why did Marian bring up these thoughts? He realized Kelly had been speaking, and he had no idea what he'd said.

"I'm sorry?" Omar adjusted his watch, feigning interest.

"I said I can't expect too much from a company whose primary language is Arabic," Kelly said more slowly, enunciating his words as if Omar might have suddenly gone deaf.

"You can't say that," Marian hissed.

"Why the hell not?" Kelly swung to look at her.

"First of all, they speak *Farsi.* Second, it's completely wrong. And finally, we are *guests* here," she said, her voice low and threatening, like a mother scolding a child in public. "You need to act like it."

"The last person I need to take direction from is you," he spat, downing his whiskey. He raised his hand, waving it in the air. "Waitress!"

Omar pinched the bridge of his nose. Tomorrow would be very interesting. Perhaps a smidge entertaining, if this buffoonery was any indicator. *Remember, treat him with respect. Even if he's deplorable.*

"We expect good things of this meeting," Omar said, measuring his words. "This company has shown interest in the idea of partnering with Almasi-Thomas, but the numbers conversation remains, of course." He paused, tapping his fingers against the tabletop. "National Oil is very hesitant to meet with almost anyone. The fact that they have invited us to *their* headquarters is very promising."

"Damn well better be," Kelly muttered, craning his neck to find the waitress. "Brought me all the way out to this godforsaken place."

Marian inhaled sharply. "Wow."

Omar felt the urge to interject, but Marian could handle it—he already sensed it. Yet another way she and Anahita were nothing alike. Anahita had been timid and quiet, almost to the point of irritating him. Marian's boldness was a breath of fresh air.

You need to stop comparing her to your dead wife.

He blinked, realizing he'd drifted off again, missing their spat entirely. Marian glared at Kelly, who was ordering another whiskey.

"I am so sorry for his...*belligerence*," Marian said, snagging Omar's gaze with wide, imploring eyes, exactly the color of honeyed chocolate.

"I am not being belligerent," Kelly huffed. "You're too goddamn sensitive. Exactly why I told Bob I didn't need him sending a woman with me on this trip."

Omar watched Kelly a moment, unsure if he'd heard him correctly. Marian's jaw dropped, and she shook her head.

"There's no need for that—" Omar began.

"You need a woman more than you can even possibly understand," Marian spat. "You are a selfish brute and completely unaware of how big of an asshole you are." She stood up from her seat, the chair nearly toppling behind her. She looked at Omar with fiery eyes, and he shrank back a bit.

"I think I'll have dinner in my room," she said, offering a hand to Omar. "Thank you for your hospitality."

Omar took her hand and glanced between Marian and Kelly. It felt as if an explosive might detonate if they remained in the same room. Kelly snorted in derision, and Marian stomped off without another word, leaving her half-drunk martini behind.

Omar shot to his feet and took off after her. The professional side of him advised him to let her go, but something else wanted her to stay.

"Marian, wait." He jogged across the brilliant tiles of the foyer as she stormed to the elevators. She didn't seem to hear him, so he moved faster, reaching for her shoulder.

She gasped and turned to him. "What?"

"You shouldn't have to leave."

Her plump lips turned into a frightening thin line. "I know. But my job here is to help broker this deal. I'll be there tomorrow, but I won't spend another second of *my* time around that pompous pig."

Marian brushed her curly hair behind her ear, revealing a pair of dangling earrings. Omar's gaze fastened onto them, admiring the sheen of blue and silver. *Butterflies.* His belly twisted violently. Anahita had a flight of blue and silver butterflies tattooed across her left shoulder.

His mouth parted, but he didn't have words.

"Just go back there and wine and dine the asshole," she said finally. "It's fine."

She turned to leave but he reached for her arm, stilling her again.

"What?" she asked again. She looked at the end of her rope, and he couldn't blame her.

"I, uh…" He cleared his throat, forcing his gaze off her earrings. "I just wanted to say that I'd much rather be dining with *you*."

Marian grinned, that same rosy flush appearing in her cheek. "Yeah, well…It would be nice, wouldn't it?" A moment of awkward silence passed, and then she started again. "I'll see you tomorrow morning."

Omar let her go this time, let himself be captivated by her petite, curvy figure as he watched her walk toward the elevators.

She was the *only* one he wanted to have dinner with tonight. And for reasons that had nothing to do with business.

CHAPTER THREE

The next morning, Marian woke up early to get herself centered. She'd spent the majority of her first night in Minarak bitching to Annabelle about Kelly's intolerable comments and gorging on decadent hotel food, so today needed to be a clean slate.

Today she was going to do her actual job, clean up the project, and get on her way to never seeing Kelly again.

She reviewed the files she'd brought for the presentation, even though Kelly was in charge of handling it and would never let her get a word in edgewise. She'd come so prepared that she could actually do Kelly's job. In fact, she would do it a million times better, given his inherent aversion to sensitivity and diplomacy.

If she liked her job less she might have found the sinking ship of Kelly more entertaining. But really, it just stung. He was ruining their good name and burning bridges around the world. Annabelle was equally aghast at his behavior, but her only warning last night for the presentation was: *be prepared to assert yourself.*

Her words rang in Marian's ears as she buttoned up her ruffled shirt, tucking it into a plain, black skirt.

Marian grabbed her sleek briefcase and purse, then headed downstairs to meet Omar and Kelly so they could carpool to National Oil's headquarters for the meeting. At least with Omar here, she wouldn't have to worry about the car departing without her. In the lobby, the two men waited by the front doors. Kelly already had a sour look on his face.

"Good morning," she said brightly, ignoring the pulse behind her eye that cynically awaited a snide comment from Kelly. As soon as Kelly opened his mouth to speak, she added, "I hope that whatever you're about to say is kind."

Kelly watched her for a moment then turned away. "Let's go."

Omar sent her a secret grin as they walked into the Minarak morning. Traffic hummed in the distance, beyond the stone walls surrounding the hotel property. The air was misty with city dew, casting a gauzy glow over everything. *This would be a perfect day to get lost with Omar and see where we end up.*

"Did you sleep well?" Omar held the back door of the car open for her as she slid inside. Kelly quickly claimed the front seat.

"I did. This hotel is lovely." Marian waited as Omar came around to the other side, working on actively ignoring Kelly's presence in the front seat. "I had a delicious, quiet meal in my room, without any irritating outside influences."

Omar's grin widened as the driver shifted the car into gear. The ride to National Oil was pleasant and mostly quiet. Omar chatted a bit, but Kelly stayed silent, thankfully. By the time they pulled up to the boxy office building, seemingly made of black mirrors and steel reinforcement, Marian was hopeful that they could pull this deal off.

Inside, a suited man led them to a large conference room. Twenty men—nearly identical in their dark suits—already sat around the table. Three empty chairs near the head of the table waited for them. Omar said something in Farsi to the group.

"If the whole meeting will be in that language, we might as well call it off now," Kelly said, adjusting his suit coat as he settled into his seat.

Marian fought a groan. "Seriously, don't start with this right now."

"Gentlemen," Omar said in a clear voice. "Thank you all for having us here today. We are honored to be here to discuss a potential deal linking our merged companies with your oil technology."

Marian looked around the room as Omar spoke. Not a single woman. This must have been what Annabelle warned her about.

Omar gave a quick introduction to the nature of their proposed deal—utilize National Oil's machinery and systems to gain access to a coveted region for mining purposes, while offering them unlimited use of Almasi Holdings' connections in return.

"Our company is the best in America," Kelly interjected, his puffy face looking more pompous than usual. "We're an invaluable link, one only idiots would turn down."

A tense moment of silence settled over the table, and Marian sensed the need to intervene. One of the oil tech men began speaking at the same time she did, though, so she subsided.

"We're prepared to let you have use of our newest line of machines," he said in slow, practiced English. He rattled off the model numbers, which Marian immediately recognized from her recent studies of machine reviews.

"Excuse me," she said quietly. When another man began speaking over her, she said again, "Excuse me, gentlemen, but those machines have consistently poor performances in all recent trials."

Several sets of dark eyes turned to her, and she looked to Kelly and Omar. Both of them avoided her gaze, so she went on. "Those machines would not be effective for our purposes," she said, adding a few figures about the scope of the mining work Almasi-Thomas intended to do.

Kelly chuckled a little, all but reaching out to pat her on the head. "Well, thanks for that."

Some of the oil tech men tittered. "Women always seem to have a response to everything, don't they?"

A ripple of laughter coursed through the room, and Marian's neck heated up. Anger prickled through her, and she turned to Omar for help. He had to see the logic here. He was sane and rational, and handsome. *Help me out here.*

"We should lock her up, like you guys do with your women." Kelly waved his hand dismissively across the table, a sneer on his face. "Isn't that right? They can barely leave the house without permission. Seems like it might work on this one."

A heavy silence thudded across the table, and Marian gaped at Kelly. *Oh. My. God.* Just when she thought he couldn't get worse, he did. The man knew no limits.

One of the oil tech men fired off something fast and angry in Farsi, to which Omar responded with a furrowed brow. A moment later, several men were shouting in Farsi, and the entire meeting had exploded before her eyes.

"What the fuck is wrong with you?" she hissed at Kelly. "Did you seriously just say that?"

"It was a joke," he shot back. "Seems nobody can take one these days. Bunch of sensitive pussies everywhere I go."

Marian let her head drop into her hands. He wasn't even worth it. He had a skull as thick as a glacier. And a brain that moved about as fast as one. A moment later, Omar stood, looking down at both of them with an intense gaze.

"We have to go." He nodded toward the door.

He led them out of the conference room, leaving a thick wake of tension behind them. In the hallway, the air was cooler and twenty pairs of angry eyes weren't boring into them. She turned to Omar, making her hands into fists so she wouldn't start wringing them.

"What the fuck just happened?"

"They're refusing to do further business with us until you apologize," Omar said, staring pointedly at Kelly. "You crossed a line with them."

Kelly scoffed. "It was a joke!"

"It doesn't matter. You spoke poorly of their families and *our* culture."

"This is *business*," Kelly said, his red-rimmed eyes narrowing to slits. "I don't give a flying fuck what your women do in their spare time. That has nothing to do with this deal."

"But respect has *everything* to do with it," Marian said, crossing her arms. "And you ruined the deal by disrespecting them."

"I'd say *you* did." Kelly stepped closer to her, a sickening heat rolling off him. "You just couldn't keep your goddamn mouth shut. You don't tell the brokering firm that their equipment sucks. God knows what your real job is here, but according to me, it's to stay *quiet*."

Marian opened her mouth to respond, but Omar stepped between them, raising a hand in the air.

"Listen. This deal doesn't move forward without a representative from each of our merged companies." He looked between Marian and Kelly, his face drawn tight. Even when he was pissed and talking to them as if they were warring children, he was drop-dead gorgeous.

"I'll be the representative then." Marian balled her fists, standing up straighter. Even at her tallest, she barely reached Kelly's shoulders, let alone Omar's. "I can do his job in my sleep."

"You're insane," Kelly said.

"Well, you're argumentative and impossible to work with," Marian shot back. "If we want the deal, either you have to apologize or I'll do it." After a second thought, she added, "And I'll do the job you *couldn't*."

Kelly laughed exaggeratedly, as if acting in a bad after-school movie. "That's hilarious."

"We'll have to take this to the CEOs," Omar said after a moment, massaging his temple. "Come on."

He walked briskly down the hallway, leading them out of the building while he fiddled with his phone, presumably to call the driver. They hadn't lasted fifteen minutes in this building before being essentially kicked out. Omar paced the lobby while he spoke with someone in anxious Farsi on the phone, his shiny leather shoes tapping softly as he walked.

Was Omar on her side? He was hard to read. He clearly was miffed about Kelly's inglorious stunt, but didn't seem very excited by the idea that she take over. Though he probably didn't have the executive function to just kick Kelly out and let her slide into his place. Still, it would have been nice to see more support from him. He'd barely looked at her in the meeting when she brought up the crucial point. If they got into a bad deal with piss-poor machinery, then what was the point?

Marian stood far to the side, arms crossed. If she could avoid speaking another word to Kelly, she would. But for the life of her, she couldn't imagine how he'd managed to snag—or keep—his job with an attitude like his. It was like he tried to sabotage himself at every turn. The business would be better off booting his ass to the curb.

A moment later, the car arrived, and the three of them got inside in tense silence. The ride to Almasi Holdings didn't feature even a murmur of conversation. Marian tapped out furious texts to Annabelle, updating her about the heinous happenings, to which her friend responded with pure "OMG"s and "WTF"s.

At Almasi, Omar practically led the two of them up to the top floor by their ears. Marian had never felt so much like a kid in trouble. Here they were, going to meet the Parsian CEO, who would report back to the American CEO. It felt exactly like tattling, and someone was about to get a painful ass whooping.

The Sheikh Almasi, Omar's father, sat stern and majestic behind an enormous desk in a lushly appointed office lined with bookcases. The air smelled faintly of myrrh.

"Father, I'd like you to meet Kelly Gunther and Marian Frank. Kelly is the CTO of our American branch, and Marian has accompanied him to finalize the deal with National Oil. We had a problem at today's meeting that is, as of now, completely unresolved."

Mr. Almasi nodded, his jowls wobbling a little. "Let's call New York, shall we?"

CHAPTER FOUR

Omar sank into a chair while his father dialed Mr. Thomas. Not only was this an epic deal-making failure, their call was timed for squarely in the middle of the night over there. Who liked to be woken up to bad news?

Kelly and Marian sat stiffly in the chairs beside him. Marian craned her head as she peered around the office, clearly fascinated by her surroundings. He liked that about her—in fact, he could watch her observe the world around her for hours and probably never grow bored. Something about her called to him, made him desperate to know more.

The phone rang several times on speaker before Thomas picked up. "Hello?"

Omar's father gave a curt introduction, and then Omar took over. "Sir, we apologize for the intrusion so late at night."

Mr. Thomas grumbled from his end of the phone.

"There was a misunderstanding at our meeting today that resulted in National Oil being unwilling to negotiate until they receive an apology from Kelly." He paused, looking over at Marian, who stared daggers at Kelly. "Kelly is unwilling to apologize for what he says—"

"Bob, I made a joke," Kelly interrupted. "These guys are so sensitive, so easily offended. They need their own safe spaces."

Mr. Thomas sighed. "Marian, didn't I send you along for just this reason?"

"Mr. Thomas, I have done everything I possibly can to reel in this arrogant and offensive *prick*," Marian said. "But he is his own man, and I cannot make his decisions for him or tape his mouth shut, as much as I would like to. He made a tasteless joke about the women of Parsabad, and I can't blame National Oil's team for—"

"You need to shut your dirty mouth right now," Kelly snapped. Omar raised a palm, as though it would quiet him. Kelly barreled on regardless. "I won't apologize to a bunch of sensitive pussies who can't even focus on business for ten goddamn minutes."

"Kelly," Mr. Thomas said from across the world, "you're tired."

Kelly's brows knit together as he sputtered in confusion. "What the hell did you say?"

"You're fired. You need to make your way back to America on your own dime. Now get the hell out of this business deal before you ruin everything."

Kelly looked between Omar and Marian before launching to his feet. "You all are a bunch of weak-willed idiots! I hope the deal fails and you all simmer in a pile of your own shit!" He wobbled out of the office. After a tense moment in the office, Omar looked at Marian to find her grinning.

"Was that funny to you?"

"I don't know what I'd call it. But I know I can breathe easier now that he's gone."

"Marian, will you handle the deal?" Mr. Thomas sighed wearily. "I should have sent you to do this job from the get-go."

"I will absolutely handle this deal to the best of my ability." Marian smiled widely at Omar and his father.

Omar glanced at his father, who nodded. "Yes. This seems like a positive movement forward. I believe my son will work well with Marian." After a moment, he added, "And this will be very good for PR, for both of our divisions."

"Will I be the first woman to broker a mining deal in Parsabad?" Marian asked.

"If you are, we'll be sure to play that up," Omar said, relaxing into his seat. She'd been right—it was easier to breathe without Kelly the nuisance in the room. But despite his own relief, he wasn't entirely sure that having Marian at the helm would work as well as everyone thought. Beneath Kelly's astounding crudeness, he'd had a point—many businessmen, especially in the Middle East, didn't listen to women.

Mr. Thomas was disconnected by default, over there in America. Omar's father was detached from the world of present-day operations, since he left the bulk of that to his sons. And ever since Annabelle had come into the family business, it seemed he'd turned over a new egalitarian leaf. And while that was commendable, it didn't make Omar's job any easier.

Because Omar still had to deal with all the chauvinistic men who populated the business world. Marian had to know too, just from working with Kelly alone. But if she were a man, their brokering might work a little better.

But if she were a man, you wouldn't be nearly as drawn to her.

A shiver coursed through him, and he forced his gaze off her wild curls. He wanted to drag his fingers through her hair, to catch the sweet scent of her shampoo. He'd been dying to grab a handful of her curves since laying eyes on her, but it still felt wrong. Both because of business and because of his late wife.

The group hung up the call with Mr. Thomas, and Omar's father clasped his hands. "I expect you'll contact National Oil to arrange a new meeting."

"Immediately." Omar stood, re-buttoning his suit coat, and waited for Marian to stand as well. In the hallway, she turned to him, those honey-chocolate eyes making his belly do a nosedive.

"Omar, I know you don't know much about me, but I'm a killer worker," she said, sounding rushed. "I do my research, and I live and breathe my job. So when I interrupted in the meeting today, I wasn't 'being a woman.'" She made exaggerated air quotes with her fingers. "I was bringing up a valid point—those machines they want to provide to us are *useless.* I'll show you the research. I think they're offering this as a way to either give us a bad deal or to make us turn away entirely."

Omar clenched his jaw, weighing her words heavily. *How to delicately explain the rules of the game?* "I see your point. And I'm glad you said something. Except—"

A happy exclamation echoed through the hallway. Annabelle hurried toward Marian, her arms outstretched, her face lit up with a contagious smile.

"It's you!" Marian shrieked and ran into her friend's arms. "I can't believe it's you, you freaking Persian Princess!"

Annabelle laughed as they hugged. Omar relished the familiar energy between the women, felt it seep into him, warming him through. He hadn't felt that sort of connection in a long time. And he liked being at Marian's side, having that energy in his proximity.

"Omar, how is this vixen treating you?" Annabelle punched his shoulder jokingly, then pulled him in for a hug. "She's smart as a whip. Though I'm sure you've already seen that."

"Yes, actually." Omar smiled at Annabelle, shoving his hands in his pockets. "She's been responsible for one firing so far, as well."

Annabelle gasped. "He's finally gone?"

The two friends chattered happily for a few moments, which Omar observed as if doing a sociological study. Not just because they were old friends, but because he wanted to learn more about Marian. He was fascinated by her quirks, the smirk that preceded certain quips, the way she brushed back her hair with a flick of her wrist, the mischievous sparkle in her eyes that told him there was a whole different layer to her he had yet to explore.

Why are you so fascinating? He looked away, as though to train his mind to ignore her. Marian was linked to his wife— maybe irrationally so—and for better or worse, he had to ignore the former because of the latter. There was no other way.

The women wrapped up their conversation once Annabelle checked the time. "I'm on my way to a meeting right now," she said, squeezing the sides of Marian's arms. "I'll text you about meeting up later. Love you, girl."

They hugged again, and once Annabelle trotted down the hall, Marian turned to him with an ear-to-ear grin.

"I had no idea you two were so close," he mused, pointing down the hallway. He led the way to his office, which was just around the corner. Her being close to Annabelle was…a relief. Somehow. Or at least exciting. There was something buried deep within that relationship that comforted him, made him distantly curious to see how things with Marian might develop.

"Oh, yes. We're sisters, without the blood." Marian snorted as he led her into his office. It was a corner office, significantly smaller than his father's but well-lit and airy. "And you're Imaad's brother…so I guess that makes us in-laws, somehow."

Omar laughed a little, sitting in front of his desk. "Yes, I suppose."

"So, what about you, Omar? We haven't gotten a chance to really get to know each other. I mean, I should know *something* about you, since we're working together now." She cocked a winning grin, propping her hands against the back of the chair facing his desk.

"Well, there's not much to know, really." He leaned back in the chair, trying to affect a relaxed air, even though this probing turn of conversation made him nervous.

"Do you have any other brothers or sisters?"

"Imaad and Zahir. That's it."

"The three heirs." Marian grinned, flicking her hair back from her face. "What about family? Kids?"

"None of those," he said, forcing a little laugh. *Please don't ask anything more.*

"Married?"

He swore there was a lilt in her voice as she asked it, which both uplifted and devastated him.

"Uh…yes." When he noticed she looked a little crushed, he added, "I was. My wife, uh…she passed away two years ago."

Silence filled the room, and Marian's face fell. "Oh, God. I'm so sorry to hear that. I didn't mean…" She nibbled on her bottom lip, shaking her head, ringlets swaying. "I shouldn't have asked."

Omar tapped his fingers on his desk, crippled with indecision. Here it was—the elephant in his head. Impossible to avoid now. And maybe this was his cue to draw the line in the sand. *Now.*

"Well, I'm going to get to work on setting up another meeting with this company," Omar said, reaching for some files on his desk.

"Great," Marian said quickly. "I'll draft a presentation, one that will address today's horrible outcome and then how to move forward from here."

Omar nodded, avoiding her gaze. "Excellent. Let's meet tomorrow."

Marian nodded and let herself out of his office, leaving a wake of confusion behind her. He stared at the door for a long time, combatting the "Wait" dangling on his lips.

CHAPTER FIVE

After an invigorating lunch with Annabelle and a productive afternoon of business planning, Marian was ready for one more self-esteem boost.

She dressed carefully in her hotel suite while on speaker phone with Layla, a friend from NYC.

"You should wear the red one," Layla said, even though she couldn't see the options being considered.

"Yeah, but that might scream something I don't want to scream in this male-dominated society," Marian said, nibbling her lip as she looked at the three dresses lying on her bed. "All I want is to look sexy for myself and have a relaxing, exploratory night out in Minarak."

"Are you sure you don't need a sexy Almasi brother on your arm?"

Marian's stomach plummeted to her feet. "Ugh. I didn't tell you." She relayed the awkward encounter earlier that day in Omar's office. "That's what I get for being forward with a business associate."

"You weren't *forward*, you were just curious."

"Yes, I know, but my intentions were forward," Marian said, snatching up the black dress. This one would do. Just the right amount of cleavage and curves.

"He can't know that," Layla pointed out.

"That's true. But I feel like he did." She sighed, shimmying out of her work clothes. "He's just so *hot*. Annabelle told me her husband was sexy, but she failed to mention how gorgeous his brother is."

"Once you're married you can't say stuff like that," Layla said.

"Bullshit. Annabelle and I don't work like that." Marian laughed as the dress settled softly over her body. She tugged it into place, admiring the tops of her breasts peeking out from the off-shoulder neckline. "If a dude is hot, he's hot. Which reminds me, you need to come work for this company."

Layla sighed. She worked for a journalism firm as a researcher. "You're always trying to recruit me."

"I know. But especially now." Marian flitted over to the bathroom mirror to touch up her makeup, making her eyeliner a little darker. She set the phone down next to the sink. "We need more women in this world. Today's failure made me realize just how badly we still need to break the glass ceiling."

"I'm just not quite ready to leave my current job," Layla said. "I think I might be getting a raise soon."

"You've been saying that for a year," Marian retorted. "If they offer you a raise, let me know the amount, and I'll make sure we beat it."

Layla laughed. "You drive a hard bargain."

"This company is like a family. It *is* a family. Well, two families." She tried to still her blinking as she traced the bottom curve of her eye. "So it's kind of like *My Big Fat Greek Wedding,* except with Parsabad. And in one of the families, you have to fight tooth and nail for everything."

"Not all families are like that," Layla said.

"Well, fine. But my point is, this is a good place to work. And sometimes there are perks, like rampant victory over assholes, and gorgeous, dark, Parsian eye candy."

"Will you sleep with him?"

"I would need his permission first, but yes." Marian blinked through an application of mascara. "Okay. I'm heading out for my little tourist night."

"I can't believe it's dinner time there. I just woke up. I'll talk to you later, girl."

The friends hung up, and Marian gathered her purse before slipping her feet into the pair of peep-toe shoes she'd brought. She didn't travel anywhere, near or far, without at least a few different sexy-night-out options. It was part of her self-care routine, something she started years ago when she realized most men were either way below her standards or way too intimidated by her. It made the dating pool laughably small, and so the best bet was to simply date herself.

Marian took the elevator downstairs and strutted out into the lobby confidently. This was amazing already. Eyes gravitated toward her, and she absorbed it all, relishing the attention. Especially after a painstaking morning of being ignored, overlooked, and undervalued.

As she passed the reception desk, a tall, broad-shouldered man stood out to her. She blinked, sizing him up from behind. A pale blue linen shirt, dark gray slacks. Thick, dark hair swept back from his face, so luscious she wanted to run her hands through it. *Is that Omar?* Marian slowed and stared at him, willing him to turn around.

Omar turned a moment later, his nervous gaze landing immediately on her. She lifted her brows and clicked her way toward him.

"Hey there!" She smiled brightly. He shoved his hands in his pockets as he approached her.

"Hi, Marian." A grin flickered on his face but failed to light.

"What are you doing here?"

Omar paused, avoiding her gaze. "Well…"

Suddenly his nervousness clicked into place. He didn't want to be caught here—but why?

"I wanted to double check that Kelly had left." Omar cleared his throat, jingling some change in his pockets. "So he wouldn't cause any issues for you. I mean, the company."

Marian nodded. "Very thoughtful of you. I was just on my way to dinner," she said, gesturing toward the front door. "Would you like to join me?"

Omar's gaze raked up and down her body, and she swore she heard him sigh. "Yes. That sounds…" He paused, something unknown crossing his face. "I actually should get home. I forgot I have to—"

"Oh, come on." She grabbed at his wrist, leading him toward the sliding front doors. Whatever his hesitation was, she'd cure him of it. "Let's go grab a bite to eat. I'm new to this city, and I need a guide. You did volunteer last night."

This seemed to ease his doubts, because he complied with her tug instead of resisting. "I'll call my driver."

"No. I want an authentic experience." She led him toward the sidewalk, her hand slipping into his. Heat flooded her like an electric shock, and she glanced back at him with surprise. Confusion shone on his face, and she squeezed his hand, pulling him faster. "Show me how to hail a cab in Minarak."

On the sidewalk, cars meandered past the hotel, a few obvious taxis approaching. Something about Omar felt new right now. Nothing like the level-headed, confident businessman she'd interacted with thus far. This man was cautious, as if he'd just arrived at a party where he knew no one.

Omar paused, appraising her heavily. Oh God. He's going to back out. He's going to run away.

Marian deflated a little, but Omar raised his arm and waved it vigorously in the air. "This is how you do it. Just quickly. Several should stop."

As if on cue, three taxis pulled over to the side of the road, and Omar smiled at her. This time it felt genuine.

"Well, thank you for that. I would have done it much more aggressively, based on my experience as a New Yorker." She picked the first taxi that approached and slid into the backseat. "Now how do I say, 'Take me to the fanciest restaurant in the fanciest district'?"

Omar laughed a little and leaned forward, instructing the taxi driver in Farsi. She caught a whiff of his cologne as he settled back into the seat.

"That's a bit too much for the first lesson," Omar said. "How about we just start simple?" He pronounced the word for *restaurant*, which he repeated a few times while she stumbled over it lamely.

"Yeah, that works," she said finally, happy that he'd decided to accompany her. Something felt natural with him, as if she were reconnecting with a long-lost friend. Even though it made no sense, and she had no basis for it...it was there.

The taxi driver pulled up to a tall building, encased in reflective blue panes. The bottom level was a restaurant—she could see the maître d's stand as a well-dressed couple entered. As she stepped out of the taxi, which Omar insisted on paying for, Marian craned her neck upward to see what lay above.

"This looks pretty fancy."

"It's just fancy enough," Omar said. "They'll let me in, at least."

"Oh, please." She waved her hand at him as they strutted toward the front doors. "You look like an off-duty underwear model."

Omar lifted a brow at the same time her words crashed around her. *Jesus, Marian, could you get a filter?* She opened her mouth to smooth it over, but found nothing waiting on her tongue.

He opened the door for her, an amused air lingering between them. As they approached the podium, his hand found the small of her back. She relished the jolt of electricity that coursed through her again, made her toes tingle.

Omar spoke to the hostess, and soon they were seated at an intimate table for two along the front windows, overlooking the busy street. The glass was tinted from the outside, so they could peep out on the world in peace.

"This will be fun," Marian said, settling into place. She smoothed the napkin over her lap in preparation. "We get to comment on everybody's fashion choices without them knowing."

"So you're a voyeur," Omar said, his eyes glinting.

"Maybe," she said, teasing. "Important things to know about your business partner."

A waiter came with glasses of water and the wine list. As Marian perused the choices, a thought occurred to her.

"Don't think you have to pay for my dinner," she said, her gaze traveling along his square jaw, over the five o'clock shadow. "You just ran into me at the hotel, so this isn't me strong-arming you into a meal. I'm on an expense account, after all."

"Please. I would hardly be a good man if I allowed a guest in my country to pay for her own meal."

Marian batted her eyes at him. There were sparks here—right? She swore there were. Or maybe he was just being a sweet host. It was so hard to tell. The only thing she *did* know was how desperate she was to peel that shirt of his off and see what lay beneath.

They talked easily while waiting for the main course. Marian sipped on wine while Omar nursed a sparkling water. When she ordered her second glass, she said, "You don't drink alcohol?"

"Not much anymore," he replied, eyeing her as she downed the rest of her wine. "I…gave it up."

"Any reason?"

A strange cloud covered his face, the same one that appeared when she'd caught him at the hotel. "Not really."

"You're just a good boy, then." Marian folded her fingers over the table, casting him a secret smile. How many more hints did she need to drop? She'd held his hand and called him an underwear model. By all rights, he should be mounting her by now. At least, he would be if they were in New York.

"Not always." He ran his thumb over the side of his glass, his dark gaze setting her pulse racing. *There it is.* The man could start a fire with so few words. That was a talent.

"Hm. You seem like a pretty good boy to me." She leaned forward, conscious of her spilling cleavage. "What's an example of you being bad?"

He wet his bottom lip, his gaze not moving from hers. She could practically feel the skin sizzling on her face. "I'm not sure I'm allowed to say. Bad boys don't share."

"Oh, jeez. Now I'm really curious. This probably has something to do with your brothers, right? I bet you three got into trouble back in the day." She cocked a smile. Fire sizzled between them. *Take the ball and run with it.*

He chuckled throatily, and at the same time the waiter arrived with their dishes. Talk about poor timing. She received her plate gratefully, something with lamb and an impossible name. Omar looked just as disappointed as she felt.

The conversation flowed back to non-suggestive things, maybe due in part to the slurping and inhaling taking place over the plate in front of her. By the time their plates were cleared, Marian was stuffed and feeling significantly less sexy in her black dress. Maybe she should have left Omar at the hotel so she could bloat and grunt in peace.

But no, he was worth the discomfort of sucking her belly in post-meal. Especially when shivers thrilled through her almost any time he even glanced her way.

"So. Now that we've finished eating...I have a question for you." She dabbed at the corners of her mouth, placing the napkin on her plate. "Do you think we can salvage this deal?"

46

"No work talk," Omar said, his firm voice feeling like a sizzling slap on the ass. "That's a rule of mine."

"Ever?"

"Outside of work," he clarified, a boyish grin covering his face. "I devote enough of my time and energy to that place; I need to draw the line somewhere."

"Hmmm. In that case…" She glanced over her shoulder. "Maybe for dessert, we should…go someplace else?"

The question hung in the air for a bit too long. Each second that dragged by felt like its own separate "no." She was crazy. She was hallucinating the attraction. She needed to stay in her lane. He was a coworker, not a booty call. Every negative thought possible crowded her mind, filling her with doubt.

"Marian." Omar wet his bottom lip again, his eyes fastened on the tabletop. "We need to keep this professional."

Regret lashed at her, forced her to pinch her eyes shut with embarrassment. What had she been thinking? The sexy fantasies featuring Omar dissipated in a puff of regret. *You're an idiot to think he'd ever want to try anything with you.*

"Right." She forced a tiny grin, trying to shake the stinging rejection. The sense that no matter how craftily she used her feminine wiles, she couldn't get the hottest man in the world to say yes to her.

The waiter came with their bill, and Omar scooped it up before she could protest.

"You don't have to—" she started.

"But I want to." Omar sent his card with their server, leaving them in a tense silence.

"Listen. I'm not trying to be a creep or anything," Marian said, eager to smooth over the blip from a few moments ago. "This won't affect our professional relationship. I need you to know that. I'm just…a fun gal. I like to go do things, get to know new people. That's all."

"Of course." Omar took a sip of water, his eyes over her shoulder. Maybe he was wishing the waiter would return immediately. "Don't worry, Marian. There's no problem."

The waiter returned a few moments later, and Marian drained the rest of her wine. She and Omar walked to the front door, but she'd never felt so awkward and bulky beside a man before. *Was this the self-esteem boost you were looking for?*

Outside, Omar hailed a cab, and again several pulled over. He spoke to a driver through the front window, then held the door open for her.

"He'll take you back to the hotel," he said with a small smile. "Have a good night, Marian. See you tomorrow morning. I'll send a car for you."

He shut the door, leaving her in a gloomy silence in the back seat.

Even though it wasn't devastating or heart-wrenching or traumatic or anything of the sort...it still *felt* like it. Because there had been a secret voice inside her, whispering that Omar was on her level. *Hoping* that someone like him might be willing to have a connection with someone like her.

Just one little thing was missing: mutual attraction.

CHAPTER SIX

Omar paced the length of his office the next morning, as jumpy as if he'd overdosed on caffeine. But he hadn't—not by a long shot—and was simply anticipating Marian's inevitable arrival.

His willpower had taken a nosedive once he'd gotten home the night before. He'd gone straight to the shower and worked himself to an orgasm that made his knees buckle, Marian's image burning bright under his eyelids. That in itself felt like a betrayal. He'd had sex since his wife passed, but nobody had had that mystifying link to Anahita like Marian did.

Marian had wife potential, even though it made no sense. They barely knew each other, were strictly work partners. But still, the core of him reverberated with this knowledge, and having anyone replace Anahita seemed a grave offense. It didn't feel right to move on when his wife had been stripped of her life. It was his solidarity pact—one way to prolong the closeness.

Someone rapped on his door, and he jolted, moving to sit at his desk. But maybe he should lean against the windows, appear aloof and pensive. He walked in a circle before settling on the desk after all. He leaned against it. "Come in."

Marian poked her head in, a bright smile at the ready. Just the sight of her made him relax.

50

"Good morning." She bounced inside, clutching files to her chest. She wore simple black slacks and a tight-fitting top, one that simply demonstrated her curves instead of allowing him a glimpse of flesh. He had to pry his eyes off the deep swell of her hips.

"You look perky." He fiddled with a pen, relishing the wash of energy that coursed between them. Was this what falling in love was like? It just happened, sideswiped you, without any warning or reason. He blinked. That was not a thought fit for the office. He should *never* think that thought again.

"Well, I am. I have a lot of perky things to show you."

Like...maybe your breasts? He had to bite his tongue to keep that comment in. She would have liked it, had he allowed their conversation to flow to the sexual territory she'd craved the night before. Like any normal man with a penis. But no—he had to have the moral hang-up. Life would be easier if he weren't bound to these rigid standards.

Marian set her files on his clear desktop, spreading papers out as she hummed. Her perfume reached him, something dusky and floral. His cock twitched in his pants.

"Did you sleep well?"

"I did, thank you. You're certainly concerned about my sleeping habits." She clicked her tongue, rearranging a few papers. "Though I suppose that's nice of you. Sleep deprivation is a very serious issue, and I would want to know if someone around me was suffering from it."

He grinned. "Just trying to do my part."

She glanced up at him, the vibrancy of her eyes ensnaring him. So much of him wanted to pin her to this desk and have his way with her. But Anahita…

"Well, I appreciate your concern. Have you been eating regularly? Urinating normally?" She eased into her seat, eyebrow cocked.

Omar blinked at her, the words settling into him, and then burst into laughter. Marian looked pleased with herself.

"We could keep a chart of these things, just to see how they progress over time," she added.

"I wouldn't be opposed to that." He gestured to an empty bulletin board by his desk. "We could put it there."

"I think this is how work colleagues truly bond," Marian said with a wink. "Monitoring bodily functions."

Omar let the laughter coat him like a glaze. It felt like the first time he'd laughed—*really* laughed—in years. It was so hard to remember the last time he'd felt this way around a woman. A stranger, basically. Because it hadn't even happened this way with Anahita. She'd been an arrangement, another wily plan of his father's. They hadn't fallen in love as much as *grown* in love.

Marian got to work explaining her new approach, pointing out some notes that she'd made and a new plan of attack. When she finished, Omar clapped his hands.

"Stunning. You really do know what you're talking about."

"I told you I could replace He Who Shall Not Be Named." She puffed her chest out with pride. "No problem."

The two worked until lunchtime, when Marian excused herself to meet Annabelle. Omar headed for a café down the road, spending his lunch reading the news and thinking about Marian. When they reconvened for work in the afternoon, Marian was breathless with excitement.

"I have some news." Marian hurried toward him, resuming her spot in the chair. "I asked a friend of mine, Layla, to look into National Oil for me. She's a researcher, and I trust her. I had some misgivings about the equipment, like I told you. Well, guess what?"

It was hard not to get caught up in her excitement. He practically shouted, "What?"

"They're being manipulated." She squealed. "She found out that Arab PetroChem has a stake in National Oil. Once they found out an American company was sniffing around for a deal,

Arab PetroChem insisted on offering the cheapest equipment possible for the mining job. Because otherwise, we'd have to go out of the country to get it, which would be way more expensive for us. The imbalance in the deal would mean serious profits for National Oil and Arab PetroChem, and almost nothing for us."

"Right. There's no other local supplier for that equipment," Omar mused.

"Exactly. But what they don't know is that National Oil also works with one of *our* affiliates in the States," Marian went on. "They get materials from a company that *we* can influence. So, I think if we bring this up and convince them that equal pressure does not a good deal make, we'll get the best deal possible for everyone concerned."

Omar's mouth parted as he took it all in. "Wow." He ran a hand through his hair, popping to his feet to look out the window. "And you have this information in some form that we can present to them?"

"It's in my email right now. I can print it if you'd like. All we have to do is connect the dots."

Omar nodded, hands on his hips as he looked at her. "Excellent. Absolutely stunning." To say he was blown away was an understatement. It was all he could do to fight through the rest of their planning session, maintaining normalcy, when really he still wanted to press her against the wall and tear her clothes off.

By four o'clock, he couldn't resist it any longer. He had to give in, just a little bit. To ease the pressure.

"Let's call it a day." He slammed a pen down, looking up at her with hopeful eyes. "I'd like to take you out for a celebratory drink."

"You mean celebratory water?" She winked at him.

"No, I think I'll have a drink myself today." He stayed away from alcohol because it usually led him to one place only: sadness and reliving the most painful memories stored in his head. But today, he felt like he might have a chance at handling his liquor. At the very least, it could help him break through his inhibitions and at least *kiss* this beautiful woman.

"Wow." Her eyes widened appreciatively. "I wonder what you'll do when we seal this deal tomorrow."

"One can only wonder." He led them out of his office, locking the door behind him. He knew exactly where they'd go: a little lounge bar near her hotel, famous for after-work cocktails for professionals in the district. When they pulled up to the bar, Marian looked like a child in a candy store.

"This is the place I want to be every day after work." She glided inside, her gaze bouncing around their surroundings. Steel beams crisscrossed the open ceiling, modular art dappling the walkways between bold patterned couches. Sleek professionals lounged casually, looking more like models than the working class, even white-collar working class.

"Minarak is trendier than I imagined," she murmured, sliding onto an open couch. Omar slid next to her, their legs brushing. He slung an arm over the back of the couch, smiling down at her. This felt right—but it would feel even more right after a drink. Already he could feel the guilt threatening at the edges, promising to steal his thunder.

"It's a fun city to live in," he said. "There's always something to do, if you can stop working long enough to do it."

"I'm a bit of a workaholic myself," she said. "It's hard not to be, as a woman in a man's world."

"You mean it's harder in the US than it is here?"

"No, it's easier in many ways. But still…" She trailed off as a waiter paused to hand them menus. "It's a fight to be taken seriously."

"I can't imagine," he said, the only thing that seemed appropriate.

"Well, apparently possessing tits means you're somehow less capable."

At the anatomical reference, Omar couldn't help but glance downward. "I'd say they make you more capable."

"Really?" A knowing smirk waited for him. "How so?"

"They attract all kinds of attention, but still you manage to succeed. If men had breasts, we would have floundered long ago." Omar paused, perusing the menu. "Probably because we wouldn't do anything other than play with them all day."

Marian burst into laughter. The waiter arrived, and they ordered two martinis. The drinks appeared quickly, and both sipped appreciatively.

"I love a good martini," Marian murmured.

"Yes, it's very nice." He ran a tongue over his teeth, enjoying the lick of alcohol through his veins. "A fitting celebration for your investigative connections."

Marian lifted a brow, looking like she wanted to add more. His admonishment from the night before probably weighed on her. It certainly weighed on him. Perhaps the low point of his career as a man—imploring the sexiest woman he'd met to keep it professional. *That has to change. Today.*

They chatted easily, about everything from current politics to literature. One drink turned into two. When he'd drained his second drink, Omar knew he had to call it a night, or they might regret it.

"I think I should head back," Omar said, signaling for a waiter to bring their check. "I don't drink often, so I have to be careful."

"Mmmm." Marian eyed him, her eyes glittering as if she knew a secret. "A man who knows his limits. What a treat."

His heart raced as he filled out the receipt and then offered a hand to help her stand. She wobbled to her feet, laughing as she stood.

"I'll walk you to your hotel," Omar said, sticking out his arm. "It's very close."

"What a gentleman," she purred. She slid her arm through his. It fit perfectly, but more than that, the weight of her at his side felt ideal somehow. Like a piece he'd been missing. Sadness tried to take its familiar path through him but he rerouted it, inviting back the sexy thoughts from earlier. He would show her how he felt…what he'd been dying to show her.

Their steps fell quietly against the pavement as they meandered back to the hotel, more like a couple that had been together for twenty years than new work colleagues. People bustled by them. When they got to her hotel, he walked her to the elevators, not letting go of her arm.

He pressed her to the wall, out of view of the lobby. She inhaled sharply, looking up at him with the sexiest look he'd ever seen in his life. Her pink lips were a breath away, but he stilled himself. His heartbeat echoed wildly between his ears.

"Marian." He dragged a hand down the side of her shirt, his fingertips desperate for more contact. "May I kiss you?"

"What happened to keeping it professional?" She murmured, brushing her lips against his. "I mean, *yes*."

He smashed his mouth against hers, a warm, fragrant kiss emerging, something so tender and sweet that his belly hurt. They kissed again and again, their tongues mingling out of curiosity, and then out of passion. He pushed his hand into the mess of her curls, made a small noise as they kissed.

"Holy shit," Marian breathed once they parted. "That was a hell of a kiss."

His chest heaved as he looked down at her, his mind swirling with lust. He needed more than that. Way more than that. And from the looks of it, she did too.

"Want to go up to your room?"

CHAPTER SEVEN

Marian and Omar stumbled into her suite, their lips forming a vacuum seal that even the most arduous navigation couldn't break. The door clicked shut behind them as they maneuvered inside, toward her bedroom, and finally onto her bed.

Marian struggled to remove clothing as they kissed but had to break the seal once to get her shirt over her head. They quickly resumed their sloppy, desperate kisses, barely missing a beat, kissing like two teens who had just discovered their lips as sensual organs.

"Marian," Omar breathed through a kiss, his hands smoothing over the exposed skin of her belly. "You are so beautiful."

"So are you." She tugged at his shirt, and he leaned back to unbutton it. She addressed his belt while he worked, eager to get to the main attraction. Screw slowness and foreplay. She wanted him *inside her*.

Omar shrugged his shirt off a moment later, revealing washboard abs and a glistening, bare chest. His skin was the color of caramel candy, one that she wouldn't mind licking from head to toe.

"You're so smooth," she murmured, running her fingers over his chest.

"I wax," he admitted with a laugh.

"You're so vain, too," she cracked, pulling him down for more kisses.

"I'm Middle Eastern," he protested, as if this had something to do with it. Marian laughed, running her hands over the ridge of his shoulders, delighting in the arcs of his shoulder blades, the hills of his biceps. The man emanated heat, and his scent awakened a primal response in her, as if his pheromones unlocked something buried in her DNA.

She tugged at his pants, and he leaned back again, unzipping without taking his eyes off her. His pants crumpled to the floor, revealing navy blue boxer briefs with a salacious bulge. He tugged her slacks down to her ankles and then slid them off, his gaze riveted to the pink scrap of underwear covering her pussy. It clenched in response, as if it knew he was gazing at it, and she fidgeted, waiting for him to get on top of her.

"Take your boxers off," she said, her voice coming out husky. He did as he was told, sliding them down over the ridge of his cock. His dick sprang free, bobbing slightly in the air. Her mouth parted as she looked at it, the thick shaft framed by tight tufts of black hair.

"Okay. Yeah. Let's do this." She tugged at him again, but he stood solidly, grinning down at her.

"Hang on." He slid her panties down, revealing her messy patch of pubic hair. Why hadn't she shaved the second she met Omar? Just in case. She was about to apologize but suddenly his face was between her legs, nuzzling for entry, and she gaped, legs splaying open as she welcomed his warm, exploring lips.

Her breath caught in her throat as he licked at her clit, suckling it slowly, dragging a finger up and down the folds. Her body tensed with the unexpected attention, and her head rolled back on the bed, eyes fluttering shut as she relished this god of a man servicing her in the most intimate way possible.

He slipped a finger inside her, probing her depths. His voice came out like a growl. "You're so wet."

"I've been looking at you all night," she gasped, grabbing a fistful of his hair. She had to open her eyes, *see* him, not just feel.

He moaned appreciatively, slurping one more time at her clit before pushing on top of her. He stilled, the hot tip of his cockhead slipping between the folds of her pussy. His face clouded over with something unknown.

"Omar," she whispered, trailing her fingers over the ridge of his collarbone. "Why do I feel like I've known you for years already?"

He blinked a few times, clarity returning to his face, like he'd rejoined the real world. "I feel the same way."

Her hands made invisible patterns over his smooth chest, where there wasn't even a hint of stubble. He rolled his hips, his cock nudging the tight nub of her clit.

"Do you have…?" He let the question hang in the air.

"I don't." Her heart hammered in her chest. "But I'm on birth control. If that helps."

He nodded, leaning down to kiss her again. And then his strong hands slid underneath her, hoisting her up. He flipped her upright and she came to rest on top of him, straddling his cock, legs bent behind her.

"Wow," she said, hooking her arms around his neck. Grinning like he'd won a prize, he nipped at her cleavage. "You show surprising dexterity."

"I know how to get what I want," he said, grabbing a big handful of her ass. "And I want you on top."

His words made her dizzy for a moment. No problem with that request. She rose up as he aligned their parts and then eased down slowly, ever so slowly. Her breath dissipated once his cockhead slipped in, starting a slow stretch that felt as divine as it did challenging. He was a big boy, or she was a small girl. Either way, she sank down slowly, carefully, never breaking the intense gaze between them.

He gripped her ass cheeks with both hands, his breath coming out in pants. "Marian."

She nodded. It felt too fucking good to describe. "I know."

Once he was buried inside her, all the way to the base of his cock, he gave a low groan and she rocked slowly, delicately, trying to acclimate to his girth. After just a few moments her pussy was primed, and she moved with confidence, starting a slow roll on top of him.

Omar breathed heavily, his eyes the color of sin. "You feel too damn good. I won't last long."

"Oh, honey," she purred in his ear, feeling the same prickle of pleasure beginning a warning churn in her core. "That doesn't matter."

She rocked and rolled, loving the way he filled her completely, all the way to her core and then some. Her clit knocked against the base of his cock as she rode him, and it wasn't long before she felt herself at the edge of the precipice.

"I'm close," she whispered. Omar groaned, rolling his hips against hers, taking one of her large breasts in his hand. He tweaked a nipple just as she crashed down around him again, and the dam broke. Pleasure spilled in waves throughout her body, a raging churn that filled every pore and cell of her being. She cried out, tensing against him as she came, wave after wave of bliss.

Omar groaned and stilled beneath her, his fingers leaving deep indents in her hips, and after a few moments their groans receded, and they were left panting together, her head on his shoulder, his fingers tracing invisible patterns over her back.

When clarity returned, she looked up at him, planted a kiss on his lips.

"That was lovely," she whispered, nibbling at his ear lobe. "And approximately a thousand times better than I imagined it would be."

"Really?" He smiled boyishly. "I knew it would be that good." He bit his bottom lip as she climbed off of him, his gaze following her ass as she plopped onto the bed. "I knew it from the second I met you."

She laughed, swatting at his arm. "Stop it." So he *had* been attracted to her. She hadn't been imagining it.

"It's true." He lay down on the bed beside her, smoothing a hand through her hair. "There's just something about you, Marian."

"Something about Marian. Almost the movie they made," she cracked, wondering as soon as the words left her lips if he'd get the American movie reference.

"Except this time the white stuff didn't end up in your hair," he joked back.

She nuzzled up to his chest, eager to hear the rhythm of his heart, at least for a little bit. Until he decided it was too much, or too long, or whatever excuse he might use to disappear from her room.

She had to enjoy this man while she could. Because something told her this would be the only chance she got.

CHAPTER EIGHT

Omar awoke with a start in the middle of the night. He lay under a sheet, different sheets than his own, in some bed that was…

He blinked, focusing on the sleeping figure beside him. *Marian.* Guilt crashed through him, and he jolted upright. What a blissful dream he'd been in. One where he'd taken a beautiful woman to bed and faced absolutely no repercussions.

But now, in his waking life, that guilt he'd tried to sidestep via martini rushed back to claim its rightful place in his mind. And it was two a.m., according to the bedside clock. He had to get back to his own place, into his own bed, into his own right mind.

Omar rustled through the darkness trying to find his discarded clothing. His body still buzzed from the epic sex, which hadn't happened once or even twice, but a total of three times in rapid succession. Apparently the both of them had been starving for it, which made him feel like a twenty-year-old again.

He grinned lazily as he dressed, recalling their bedroom romp. Marian was easily his favorite lover; things just felt natural with her. Easy.

A little bit too easy, actually. He felt his way toward the door once he was dressed, leaving as quietly as he could. He winced as he hurried down the hallway, heading for the side door. This was sure to look bad, especially if a night receptionist spotted him. Marian was well-worth it, though.

*   *   *

Back in his apartment, Omar struggled to fall asleep. Instead, he tossed and turned, tortured by images of the amazing sex with Marian and feeling as if he'd let himself down somehow.

After his wife's death, he'd made himself a promise: nothing serious for a long, long time. He could have one-night stands when he needed, just for simple physical purposes, but anything beyond that would be inappropriate. The bond that he and his late wife had created during her illness forged a new moral code in him, one that he still struggled to understand. They'd loved each other deeply in the final days, and seeing her rapid loss of health sometimes felt like they'd lived fifty years together in the span of only one. He still grappled with that sense of loss, that intense closeness forged in grief. Two years felt like nothing—and yet an eternity.

The pact had worked—until Marian. She'd only been here for a few days, would only be here for a few more, but the time they'd spent together felt cataclysmic; she'd shaken the foundations of everything he believed in.

And he couldn't figure out if that was good or bad.

When his alarm finally went off, he rolled out of bed with a groan, his head somewhere between bleary and amped up. He readied for work with a strange pep in his step, no matter how hard he tried to fight it. Maybe the impromptu romp the night before would be good luck for their meeting with National Oil.

Omar returned to the hotel at nine a.m. on the dot, finding Marian already downstairs, lingering by the doors. She wore a simple skirt with a conservative button-up blouse, hiding those beautiful breasts he'd held in his hands the night before. A grin filled his face. He couldn't fight it for the world.

"Hey there." She swayed a little as she approached him. "Sleep well?"

"Sort of." He squeezed her shoulder, an automatic response he couldn't control. He just had to touch her. "I left early so it wouldn't be scandalous this morning." He nodded toward the reception desk behind them. "People talk about my family."

Her brow shot up. "Oh? That's unfortunate."

He guided her toward the car, pressing his hand to the small of her back. He caught a whiff of her perfume again.

"Are you ready to win this deal?" he asked as she slid into the backseat of the car.

"I was born ready."

He stepped to the other side of the car, taking his place next to her. Their knees knocked, and they shared a private smile.

On the ride to National Oil, he fought the urge to hold her hand. It seemed natural, as if maybe she wanted to do the same. Instead of reaching for each other, they covered some of the points of their new presentation again, rehearsing them just to be safe.

When they arrived at the boxy office building, Omar was bursting with confidence. He hadn't felt this good about the deal ever, and it came strictly from the fact that Marian was at the helm alongside him. They strolled into the building, an assistant leading them back to the same conference room where the blowout had occurred days before. Inside, the same twenty pairs of eyes greeted them. Marian passed out packets of information to each person before sitting down next to Omar.

"Hello again, gentlemen," Omar began, using the clearest voice he could muster. "We're here to present our proposed deal on behalf of Almasi-Thomas."

He went over the bones of the original deal and expounded upon the areas that had been modified since their first meeting. Marian added the data about the poorly performing equipment, gracefully mentioning the business links of both companies that would cause the original deal offered to be a bad deal for all involved.

Omar rounded up the presentation with some strong selling points, reiterating Marian's links to the outside companies, and when they were done, silence fell over the room.

A few men nodded as they looked around at each other.

"We appreciate your presentation," one said. "Including the absence of the other man."

"We appreciate it as well," Marian said.

"We'll take some time to look over the information here and have our decision by the end of the day."

Omar nodded respectfully and then waited for Marian to lead the way out of the room. Once the door shut behind them, they looked to each other with hopeful grins.

"I think we nailed it," she whispered as they stepped into the elevator. "It went off without a hitch."

"You're right. They've got to accept it," Omar said.

"I can feel it in my bones," Marian said, her heels clicking over the tiled lobby floor.

While they awaited Omar's driver, a thought occurred to him. "If we won't get the decision until the end of the day, how about taking a little trip?"

"And skip work?" She feigned incredulity then smiled. "I think that's a great idea. I'm the foreign dignitary, after all."

He laughed, slipping an arm around her, bringing her close to him. The move made her inhale sharply, and clarity slapped him in the face. What had gotten into him?

"Sorry," he said, loosening his grip. "You're hard to stay away from."

"That's what they all say," she said wryly, pushing at his shoulder. "But you should know I don't mind one bit."

"Then it's decided. We will go on a sightseeing mission. Absolutely part of today's work itinerary." The car pulled up, and he helped her into the backseat then joined her. "In fact, I know just the place we'll go."

He reached for his phone, excitement thrumming through him. He had a brilliant idea, one that would serve as an early celebration of either success or failure.

"Hopefully we'll get good news at the end of our field trip," Marian said.

"I bet we will," he said, scrolling through his phone for a friend's number. "This feels like the best day ever."

CHAPTER NINE

Marian blinked up at the massive balloon before her, unable to fully register what the plan was.

"So, you're saying..." She looked around, double-checking their surroundings. They'd left the city and stopped in an open park area. "You're saying we're going up in this thing?"

Omar nodded like a kid eager to show off his science project. "Yes. I know how to fly it."

"You're a hot air balloon pilot?"

He grinned. "Of course."

The assistant at the hot air balloon port, or whatever it was called, readied some weights near the basket as Omar opened the flimsy swinging door, beckoning her to join him. "Come on. You're going to love it."

She eyed the woven basket, trying to judge its safety without actually setting foot inside it. "What if it goes up and never comes down?"

"Impossible. Because of science."

She hesitated. "What if the balloon pops?"

"Won't happen, because today is the best day ever," Omar responded.

"It could very quickly turn into the worst day ever," she said, pressing a foot inside the bottom of the basket. It seemed sturdy enough. "Sometimes fate likes to play ironic jokes like that. You think it's the best day ever because you nailed the deal, but then the hot air balloon gets stuck in the desert and the oil tech firm calls to tell you they hated the deal and suddenly, somehow, we also owe them a million dollars."

"Wow." Omar urged her inside the basket, basically bucking her with his hips. "Is that how your mind works?"

"I'm a natural-born pessimist." She gripped the edges of the basket, avoiding the center for some reason. It just seemed to make sense. "Or maybe I'm just a Murphy's Law adherent."

"What's Murphy's Law?" Omar untied some of the ropes tethering the basket to the ground. The basket jolted beneath them.

"It means whatever can go wrong will, and at the worst possible moment." She squeezed her eyes shut as her stomach lurched. She'd never been in a hot air balloon before. It just wasn't one of those things that seemed wise. But for Omar's sake, she'd tough it out.

Even if it meant ingloriously puking from the side of a floating basket hundreds of feet in the air.

"This is perfectly safe," Omar said, sliding his hand over her shoulder. She relaxed a little. His touch certainly had a tendency to soothe. He just might have to touch her for the entire duration of the trip.

"Nothing is perfectly safe, though," she pointed out.

"You're right. But I've gone up hundreds of times. Often by myself. Today is not the day we're going to end up in the desert owing National Oil a million dollars."

He planted a quick kiss on her lips, leaving her stunned and enthralled. Hot air ballooning certainly brought out a different side of Omar. He untied the last rope and opened the propane valve. A blast of flame shot up into the balloon. He left it open in long bursts, the tssss, tssss punctuating their ascent into the sky.

Marian gripped the edge of the basket, afraid to look down but also afraid to look up. Couldn't the fabric catch on fire? She kept her eyes on the horizon, which looked like a postcard, something innocuous and surreal, sandy dunes rolling toward a cityscape.

"You like it?" Omar's eyes were wide.

"Yeah." She swallowed hard. Her knuckles had turned white. "It's, uh, different."

Omar turned up the burner, which took them higher up into the sky. Wind currents jostled the basket as they rose, sending Marian's stomach lurching. But after a few moments, the basket steadied, and they drifted effortlessly through the air. Omar slipped an arm around her, surveying the horizon.

"This is the sweet spot," he said, his voice soft and reverent. "The place where things just seem…fine."

Marian blinked, finally daring to look around a bit. The world beneath them stretched away like a fairytale: jagged, scorched mountains to the east, a glittering gulf to the south, the skyscrapers stretching up into the clouds behind them.

"It's amazing," she said, trying to immortalize this view in her head, to remember this moment forever. The best, most intangible, souvenir from her trip.

Omar sighed, running his thumb over the knotted braiding of the basket edge. "I used to come up here a lot when my wife was ill."

Marian's chest tightened at the mention of his wife. She'd forgotten about that detail, and the realization crashed around her. She looked up at him, unsure what to say.

"And then a lot more once she passed," Omar went on, a familiar clouded look coming over his face. He stared out at the day, seemingly lost in his own thoughts. Marian waited for him to continue, but he didn't go on.

"I can see why this would be nice in a time like that," she said quietly.

"She had cancer," Omar said. "It came on so fast. She was diagnosed just a few weeks after we got married. We didn't have much time together."

"How long did you date before you got married?"

Omar smiled sadly. "It was an arranged marriage. My father's suggestion."

Marian tried hard to swallow her surprise. Annabelle's own brush with an arranged marriage sounded like something out of a movie, but to think that Omar had actually done it! Be sensitive. Be calm.

"I know it sounds…crazy," Omar said, raising a hand as though to combat the thoughts she hoped he hadn't picked up on. "But it was fine. She and I had known each other for years as acquaintances. Our families are close. So it worked well."

"But did you…" Marian stopped herself before blurting out something insensitive. She'd rather die than be another Kelly. "I mean, did you have feelings for her?"

"Sure, after some time." Omar rubbed his thumb over his palm in a slow, methodical circle. "We loved each other very much. Her illness brought us together, ironically. So we savored every moment we had."

A painful silence consumed the air between them. Marian let his words hang in the air as she studied the shiny waters of the Gulf.

"I don't talk about her much," Omar went on. "My family doesn't bring her up anymore. They just act as though I'm a regular bachelor. My father has suggested another marriage, but it wouldn't be right."

Marian's skin prickled. Was this the let-down speech she'd been dreading? The you're-really-great-but-I-just-can't-right-now talk she'd heard in varying forms her entire life?

"Do you want to be a regular bachelor?"

Omar met her gaze briefly. Sadness filled his dark eyes, and for a moment, she regretted the question.

"Sometimes. But I just don't know."

Marian reached for his arm, letting her hand slide down to meet his. They clasped hands, his warmth rooting her to her spot. She didn't quite understand what had prompted the sharing on his part, but it was a sweet moment anyway. Even if she could sense the rejection coming from a mile away.

"You remind me of her," Omar said, his voice so quiet she thought she'd misheard him. "I mean, you two are nothing alike. But there's something about you."

"Something about Marian," she cracked.

Omar grinned. "Right. Your energy...I don't know. It's nice."

She offered a small smile, squeezing his hand. "Well, that sounds good." At least you're not telling me that the orgasms last night were a mistake.

Omar sighed heavily, like shaking off the mood. "I'm sorry if that was too much. I don't know why I told you all that, to be honest."

"It's okay." She dragged her fingertips up his arm, under the cuff of his short-sleeve shirt. "I like getting to know you. Even though I feel like I already know you."

He smiled, slipping his arm around her waist. The basket drifted noiselessly through the blue sky, and they leaned against the edge.

"What I should be talking about is whether you're a fan of the hot air balloon," Omar said, looking down at her. The sparkle was back in his eye. "Do you want to pilot it? We're sinking a little."

She jolted upright. "Sinking? Is that normal?"

"Yes, of course. We need to either give it more flame or let it continue to float downward." He guided her hand toward the propane valve in the center. "Want to try?"

She grimaced as she tugged the lever like she'd watched him do. The flame flicked up quickly then subsided when she let go.

Omar laughed. "Great. Now do it longer."

Marian pulled the lever again, letting the flame roar up into the vast arena of the balloon.

"You're a pro," Omar said, his hands sliding down the curve of her hips. "It's pretty sexy."

Marian lifted a brow. "Is that all it takes to turn a man on? Playing with fire?"

Omar bit his bottom lip, pulling her against him. Their hips knocked together. "See for yourself."

Marian felt what he was talking about before she saw it, the thick ridge of his cock pressing against his dark slacks. She grinned—men were so easy—and rubbed her crotch against him.

"What are you getting at? You better not think for a second you'll get me rocking and rolling in this rickety basket."

Omar grinned devilishly. "No, of course not." He spun her at the hips, pressing her belly-first against the edge of the basket. Her breath caught in her throat. She gripped the edges as he rolled his groin against her ass, his body seemingly pouring heat into her.

"We can do it this way," Omar murmured into her ear, his voice almost a growl. He moved his hips in a slow circle. Her eyes fluttered shut. "Taking in the sights."

A shuddery sigh escaped her. "Yeah, that sounds fine."

Omar's big hands moved over her waist, down to the front of her pants. He unbuttoned them, and they dropped to her ankles. He pushed her panties down, inviting the cool breeze to meet her ass cheeks.

"Yesss," he said, palming the roundness of her ass. His belt buckle clacked as he undid it, and a moment later his warm, bare cock pressed at the seam of her ass cheeks.

"Mmmm." Her head dropped as he rubbed his cockhead over the crease of her pussy. The glorious sensation distracted her from worrying about looking down.

"What a lovely way to spend the afternoon," she murmured a moment later as he placed soft kisses along her neckline. His hands pressed up under her shirt, wedging underneath her bra, firmly clasping each breast in his hands.

"I agree," he said, his voice husky. His cock slipped between the folds of her pussy, and she arched her ass toward him so he could press further. And then he slipped inside of her, breathtakingly slowly, stretching her out as he pushed deeper. She gasped, clutching the edge of the basket as his own grip tightened on her breasts. He moaned low as he plunged deeper, burying himself inside, the two of them pressed to the edge of the basket like the most erotic sightseeing tourists.

"God, that's amazing," she gasped out, once he had wriggled into the last inch of space. When he filled her, her entire body buzzed with happiness. As if he was more than just a hot partner on a business trip. As if somehow, he was meant for her.

"Mmmm." Omar rocked his hips in a slow circle, his breath hot at her ear. He tweaked a nipple as he did. She let her head fall back against his chest, tendrils of pleasure beginning to unfurl deep inside her.

A light breeze danced across her face, and between the powerful thrusts, she managed to open her eyes and catch cerulean skies, sandy stretches of shoreline. Omar grunted as he worked her. Her breath hitched as the climax came on. She groaned as he picked up the pace, moving a hand from her breast to the V of her legs, a fingertip seeking the tight nub of her clit.

He pinched at it and rolled it between his fingers. She squealed as the orgasm built and then broke through the barrier, washing her body with light and heat and pleasure. Marian quaked in his arms as she came, jerking as the waves subsided. Omar pushed in one more time, stilling against her as a groan drifted from his lips.

The two stood there, breathing heavily against each other. Marian clutched at his bicep, her gaze riveted on the Gulf below.

"Did we really just fuck in a hot air balloon?" She looked back at him, finding amusement in his eyes.

"I don't know." He slipped out of her, squeezing an ass cheek as he did. "We should probably try it again just to make sure."

CHAPTER TEN

Omar woke up early the next morning. Something nagged at him, had been there all throughout the previous evening, following him into his dreams, and now into the next day. He blinked, staring up at the white ceiling of his penthouse, silk sheets splayed around him.

Was it the deal? He and Marian should have heard from National by the close of business the day before, but amid all their sightseeing, neither had noticed that the call never came. He sighed heavily, draping an arm over his eyes.

He wished Marian were at his side. Was that the nagging feeling? He pushed to sitting, staring at the bedside clock. Six a.m. Too early for a Saturday. Especially considering how wiped out he'd been after their day together: laughing, exploring, making love…

His belly cinched. There it was again. The feeling. But was there any other way to describe what he had done with Marian? He might not love her, but they certainly weren't fucking. They made love—there was something intimate and loyal there. Even if neither had spoken the words.

He pushed out of bed, rubbing at his eyes on the way to the bathroom. He hadn't spent the night again, fearing a scandal. But every part of him wanted to stay with her, to wake up with that soft body in his arms, those curls pressed to his face.

Omar grunted as he peed, feeling both alert and sleepy. He stumbled back to his bedroom, intent on getting a few more hours of rest before beginning his day. He had no plans, but he had a feeling something would lead him to Marian.

He lay in bed, drifting in and out of daydreams that segued into sleep. He jolted awake just before eight when a text message came through.

"You awake?" It was Marian. He scrambled to answer it, typing out a fast response.

"I am." He sent the message, staring at his words. There was so much more he wanted to say. A moment later, his phone rang. He smiled as he answered it.

"Good morning, beautiful." It felt good to say those words and mean it.

Maran laughed on the other end of the phone. "You certainly woke up in a generous mood."

"I'm being honest, not generous," he said, fluffing the pillow beneath his head. "Why are you up so early on your day off?"

"Well, I had an idea and thought you might like to join."

"What's that?"

"Sightseeing!" Marian's tinkling laugh delighted him. "Wanna come with?"

"Yesterday's sights weren't enough for you?" He rolled out of bed, heading for his closet. Of course he'd go. It was exactly what he'd been hoping for.

"I couldn't see too many sights through the orgasms," she said. "But I appreciated the effort."

He chuckled, pulling a linen shirt from the closet, followed by a pair of light gray pants. "Should I come soon?"

"As soon as you can," she purred. "And anywhere you'd like, too."

He paused as her words sank in, then he laughed. "Naughty girl."

"I'll be here. We can have breakfast together before we go, if you'd like."

He smiled, excitement prickling through him. "I'll be there in a half hour."

When Omar strolled into Marian's hotel, she was already waiting for him in the hotel's restaurant. She waved at him from a corner table, bread plates and glasses of orange juice crowding the table.

"I got you an American breakfast," she said. "I kinda miss it. So I thought we could share it."

He pulled back his seat, admiring the spread. A waffle stared up at him from the center of the table. "I think that's a lovely idea."

"Have you ever had waffles before?" She pointed her knife at the puffy monstrosity. "There's a certain technique to eating them. It includes a half pound of butter." She licked what looked like jelly off the knife.

Omar unfolded the napkin over his lap, taking a sip of the orange juice at his setting. "Yes, but only once. And I'm certain that I didn't eat them correctly. They were plain."

Maran's jaw dropped. "Waffle faux pas!"

The two chattered happily as they barreled through the breakfast spread. Marian kept him laughing and eating, way more than he normally would at such an hour. He liked sharing in this slice of her home culture…and even more, he liked just *being* with her. Besides, he was inclined to do almost anything she suggested. If she'd implored him to take a bite of a stale rice nugget, he would have done it.

"I'm stuffed," he said after finishing off the plate of eggs. He folded up his napkin, setting it on the empty plate. "We better start sightseeing, or else I'll fall asleep."

"Agreed. So I have a list of must-sees." Marian produced a little slip of paper, smoothing it over the table top. "Based on some research and my own morbid curiosity."

Omar studied the list, which had at least fifteen items on it. "The catacombs." He noticed but didn't mention the butterfly garden on the list. That connection again...

"I've heard so much about them! Anyway, since you're the resident Minarak native, you have to be the tour guide."

"Of course. I promised." He flashed a smile, snatching up the paper. "I like this. I don't think I'll even tell you where we're beginning."

They rose from their seats, Marian's jaunty smile practically a drug for him. "Just don't lead me down any dark alleyways."

"Not even for my own selfish purposes?" They fell into step beside one another as they headed for the front doors. He wanted to sling an arm around her, but there were too many eyes at this hour in the grand hotel foyer.

"Those are the only allowable purposes," Marian said, knocking her shoulder against him. They shared a private smile, one that sent a jolt through him. This was going to be as good a day as yesterday, if not better. And his companion had everything to do with it.

The doors slid open as they approached, and a puff of dry summer air reached them. He paused by the curb as he texted his driver to pull up. Marian slid a pair of sunglasses onto her nose, surveying the day with her hands on her hips.

"If there's one thing I accomplish in Parsabad during my stay," she said, "It's going to be brokering the damn deal. But the close runner-up is going to be a slew of cringe-worthy tourist photos, so I hope you don't mind a selfie stick." She patted the oversized purse on her arm with an evil grin.

Omar laughed as the car rolled up. He held the back door open for her, more excited than he'd ever thought possible at the notion of a selfie stick. It was one of those things that didn't figure into his regular life. But with Marian at his side, it only felt right. And the idea of documenting this day, their time together, this brief and joyful respite from his regular life, was a welcome one.

He spoke quickly to the driver then slid into the back seat with Marian, his arm immediatcly settling over her shoulders. He grabbed her chin between his fingers, tilting her head to look back at him.

"Why are you the only woman who can make a selfie stick sexy?"

Her cheeks flushed. "Well, it depends what pictures we take, but…"

He brushed his lips against hers as the car rolled into motion. They had a whole day and a whole list ahead of them. And already Omar wished it would never end.

*   *   *

The two spent their day gallivanting through Minarak from east to west, north to south, imbibing every manner of touristy sightseeing opportunity available. The catacombs started off their morning, followed by a morbid tour of a famous cemetery, climbing to the cupola of a supposedly haunted unused mosque, lunch at a traditional Parsian buffet, tasting the chocolate treats of three separate famous dessert shops, and the butterfly garden. Her delight as the flying bits of color flocked to her cup of nectar had in turn delighted him. They ended with dinner and an old-timey Parsian movie with no subtitles, totally at Marian's insistence.

By the time the movie let out, it was after dark. They walked down the sidewalk in a pleasant silence, Omar feeling entranced by the events of the day. The movie had left him with some interesting things to ponder, one of the most potent being the realization that he'd felt *relaxed* all day.

When was the last time he could say that for himself? He'd never felt so at ease with anyone before—certainly not a lover— not even Anahita. Their entire day had passed in a delightful blur, leaving him wanting more time with Marian, more of *her*.

Her arm rubbed against his—their version of holding hands for the day. "Whatcha thinking about?"

"That movie." He scuffed his heel against the cement sidewalk as they strolled. "I wish there had been subtitles. It really made me think."

"I could tell there was some heavy stuff going on," Marian remarked, the glinting streetlights highlighting the streaks of gold in her hair. "But I was mostly focusing on the sounds, and that impeccable 1960s makeup."

Omar shoved his hands into his pockets. "Well, those two guys were trying to save the rich man the whole time. He wanted to commit suicide."

"So who was the beautiful lady?"

"His dead wife." Omar cleared his throat. "She wanted him to move on. But he just wanted to die to be with her."

Marian nodded as they strolled, her gaze on the ground. "Interesting."

A long silence followed them, one that felt painful somehow. Omar wasn't sure if the things on his mind were also on Marian's.

"You know, it's a well-timed movie choice," she said, her voice breezy. "The man chooses to move on. Just like you've moved on from your past, too."

Her words echoed inside his head, each repetition making him feel queasy. She nudged him after a moment, smiling up at him.

"Right?"

Omar swallowed a knot in his throat. Moving on wasn't in the plans, not this soon, not so fast. Guilt flooded him, made his knees wobble for a moment, and he inhaled sharply, trying to regain the lighthearted mood from only moments ago.

"I don't know." He fished out his phone, messaging his driver to meet them. The day had already come to a natural close—and this was more of a sign than ever that he needed to retreat. He'd gone too far. He at least needed the solitude to think about what he was doing—what he was *feeling*. Nothing made sense suddenly. Hearing the truth from her lips felt like an unexpected punch in the gut.

"Are you calling the driver?" Marian looked a little crestfallen.

"I did." He forced a smile. "It's getting late, don't you think?"

"Yeah." She looked around, gnawing at the inside of her lip. "We did accomplish a lot from the list."

"Over ninety percent of it in one day, which is more touristy things than I've done in my entire life."

A smile flickered on her face, as the car pulled into a side alley in front of them. They walked there quietly, a heaviness between them. *All your fault.* He'd ruined the good vibes in one fell swoop, but what else could he do? A simmering mood encroached quickly, and he needed the alone time to figure it out.

Inside the car, Marian nestled up to him. He slung his arm around her shoulders, but didn't press further.

"So." She tilted her head back to look at him, her brown eyes illuminated by the passing lights of downtown. "Are you sure there isn't anything else on the agenda?"

He smiled but couldn't find the words to respond.

"The hidden agenda?" She poked his side, waiting for a response. "Any agenda at all?"

He feigned tiredness, looking over at her with a regretful smile. "I don't think we should pursue the hidden agenda tonight. I need to be up early tomorrow."

Her face fell, which lashed at him. "Oh. Well, that's fine." She pulled away a little, turning to look out the window. "What's going on tomorrow?"

"I have a few family obligations," he said, which wasn't a lie. Every Sunday he met with his brothers and father and other relations for lunch. Annabelle would be there, which he remembered only after the words had left his mouth. Marian could find out about the Sunday family meet-up easily enough. *But wouldn't it be nice to bring her along?*

His stomach twisted violently. He needed to process this conflict alone.

"Well, thanks for the great day." She patted his knee like a mother would to a small child.

"Thank *you*," he said, squeezing her knee. He didn't want this to be the end of their day, but it had to be. "I had a great time."

Her eyes were full of doubt as she looked at him, his own confusion reflected back to him.

CHAPTER ELEVEN

Marian woke up on Sunday and pouted. It wasn't terribly mature of her, but she needed it. She ordered an extra-large mimosa and pancakes from room service—*Part of my self-care routine, right?*— and drew a bath in the hot tub so she could pout some more.

Omar's weird mood at the tail end of their fabulous day together left a bitter taste in her mouth, one that tasted and smelled exactly of rejection. *Why does he do this?* She wanted to shake her fists at the sky and scream it from the mountains. On the one hand, he felt like a natural companion—someone who could even be a *partner* someday. Like a real-life romantic equal. But then shit like this flared up, reminding her of the sorry truth.

Omar lived in Parsabad, he would never be her partner, and his wife was the ghost elephant in the room who just wouldn't go away.

With those factors operating against her, what was she even hoping for? Omar had to be a work colleague and nothing more. And that needed to start today.

Marian took the pancakes and mimosa into the bathroom, leaving her phone on silent in the bedroom. Part of her decision to pout and process involved not texting Omar at all and masturbating at least once, but not to his memory. Or maybe only slightly to his memory. Because the man was a sex god, and she'd probably never find his equal again in life.

Ugh. Why does he have to be so hot and good? She slipped into the warm water, pouting more, and then carefully reached for her pancakes. She leaned against the tub wall, balancing the plate along the edge, and shoveled small squares into her mouth while she angrily studied the tiles of the bathroom floor.

It just didn't make sense. She'd brought up his wife in an attempt to make that final, glaringly obvious link. He was moving on, which was evident by the way in which they hung out together. *Or wasn't it?*

She sighed, stuffing another syrupy stack of squares into her mouth. These were almost better than back home, which seemed illegal somehow. How could Parsabad do American pancakes better than a New York diner?

They do men better, too. Except maybe they didn't. She'd found the one professional and personal equal, and he just happened to still be in love with someone else. Not that she could blame him. But damn, the mixed signals were infuriating. She'd thought that their sex, at least, had been a strong enough indicator of...*something.*

She took a sip of the mimosa and then took a gulp. She'd be ordering plenty of these today, and probably lying in bed a lot too. Why did this feel like breaking up? She'd known Omar for less than a week, and yet it felt like they were ending a months-long courtship.

Sex had probably made things muddy and awkward. It always did—as a thirty-two-year-old, she should know this by now. Age didn't matter when dealing with men. It was always confusing and just this side of a shit show, no matter how mature, no matter what part of the world.

"Ugh." Marian finished the last of her pancakes and set the plate on the tiled floor. Then she sank back, letting the warm rush of water overtake her, basking in the churn of the currents.

*   *   *

A few hours later, she was awoken from a nap by the buzzing of her phone. She'd collapsed onto her bed after her skin went wrinkly in the tub, and she must have passed out soon after. She scrambled to find the phone on the bedspread. Only a few shafts of light peeked through the heavy curtains she'd left drawn from the night before.

When she found the phone, she sighed, turning it over tensely. She'd wanted to disconnect today, but already she was being a slave to her device.

Layla. Three missed calls.

Marian furrowed a brow, swiping her phone open. Three missed calls and one urgent text saying *"CALL ME ASAP."* Marian called Layla and leaned back onto the bed, yawning.

"Jesus, where have you been?" Layla sounded rushed. Cars honked in the background.

"I just woke up from a nap." Her gaze traveled to the nightstand. Six thirty p.m. "It's been a rough Sunday."

"Well, listen. I have some news." Layla's breath sounded short, like maybe she was speed walking across Manhattan. "I've been keeping tabs on National Oil since we last talked, and there has been a suspicious recent arrest on their premises."

Marian furrowed a brow. "Okay."

"Does the name Kelly Gunther ring a bell?"

"Oh God." Marian's stomach sunk. "Are you fucking serious?"

"Yeah. That asshole was taken off their property Friday afternoon. Some of the reports I found mention what seems to be corporate secret leaking."

"How do you find this stuff out?"

"I'm an investigator with security clearance," Layla said, sounding justifiably haughty. "This is my *job.*"

"Well fuck." Marian pressed a hand to her forehead. Kelly heading for National Oil after being fired from Almasi-Thomas didn't bode well. There were no *good* reasons he would show up there, either. Maybe this interference was why National Oil hadn't called with a decision on Friday. Maybe he'd made an even bigger ass of himself and made National hesitant to move forward. "Anything else I should know about?"

"I looked up Kelly's recent travels, and it looks like he's probably still right under your nose, wreaking havoc. He was released by the police yesterday."

Marian's chest tightened, and alarm bells went off. This had to be handled—immediately. If only to find out what Kelly was intending to do while in Parsabad. He should have left the country after being fired. But this move was probably him giving the middle finger to Almasi-Thomas.

"If he ruins this for us…" Marian didn't even want to finish the sentence. "Selling out" wouldn't even begin to cover it. Best case scenario, Kelly's actions would make National Oil question Almasi-Thomas's operations. He could leak all the sensitive details of their business to National Oil, completely derailing the progress they'd made. Worst case, National would pull out altogether and blackball Almasi-Thomas in the region.

"Well, now you know, and I'm positive you'll do exactly what you need to do." Layla made a kissy noise through the phone. "But I gotta run. Talk to you later!"

The line went dead, and Marian stared at her bedspread in disbelief. The pit in her stomach had morphed into a black hole. And the only thing that might make it better was immediate action of some sort.

Marian nibbled on her lip as she toyed with the idea of calling Omar. It had been her one rule for the day—no contact—but this? This was different. This was business. This was *urgent.* And it would look bad if she waited until business as usual the next day to bring it up.

She swiped to their message thread and shot off a new text. *"Hey, you around? Call me ASAP."*

The message showed as "Delivered" and then "Read" within seconds. Good old Omar with his phone always in hand. She gnawed at the inside of her lip, waiting for the phone to ring.

But it didn't. She considered sending another text, but saying what? "Urgent urgent business not about your penis, please answer"?

Marian switched to the thread with Annabelle, opting for a lighthearted check-in. *"Hey girl. How was your Sunday?"*

Annabelle responded a moment later with a photo. It was her and Imaad smiling brightly in the foreground, with a slew of Imaad's family members around a table in the middle and background, each in various states of conversation or reaction. A surprise selfie around the Parsian table. Marian smiled, zooming in to see if she could spot Omar.

There he was—toward the back. His face sullen and clouded. She huffed.

"Was that the weekly lunch you're always telling me about? Omar looks like he's having a blast."

Annabelle's response was quick. "Yeah, he was a grouch today. Left a few hours ago."

Marian reread her words a few times, an idea burbling to life. If all else failed, maybe she could swing by Omar's house to let him know about the turn of events. That way, they could start planning immediately.

"Did he go home?" Marian frowned after she sent the text, feeling a little like a stalker.

"Pretty sure. He left with Zahir."

Marian tapped the edge of her phone as she thought. *Just go for it.*

"Weird question, but could you pass me his address? Something urgent came up with the deal today, and I need to talk to him ASAP."

Annabelle sent over his address a moment later, which showed him to live just a few blocks from the hotel. *Perfect.* If he didn't call or text soon, she could swing by and just see if he was around. The information from Layla warranted a drop-in, at least…and seeing him again wouldn't hurt.

Even though you swore to keep it professional twenty minutes ago. She rolled off the bed, searching for a set of clean, casual clothes. The truth tugged at her as she dressed.

She wanted Omar in a way she could barely even articulate. And if a Sunday business call was all she could get with him…well, she'd take it.

CHAPTER TWELVE

Omar sat on his couch, running his thumb over the rim of his whiskey glass. Zahir stood at the bar by the bay windows, filling his own glass for the second time.

"Why do I feel like there's still something you haven't told me?" Zahir looked back at him, one dark brow arched accusingly.

Omar sighed. He'd asked Zahir to come back to his penthouse to discuss some matters, but still hadn't made it to the most pressing issue: Marian.

"Because I haven't told you yet." Omar set his glass down and then ran his hands through his hair. He'd wanted his older brother here specifically for his wisdom, even though Zahir had never had a serious relationship in his entire life. Still, he trusted Zahir to offer clarity. Or at least a push in the right direction.

"Well, tell me then." Zahir rejoined him on the couch, crossing an ankle over his knee. He sipped at the whiskey. "Or do I have to beat it out of you?"

"I think I'm falling for Marian." The words tumbled out of Omar's mouth, and he clammed up after he'd said them, afraid to meet his brother's gaze.

Silence settled as his brother nodded slowly, clearly mulling over the admission. "Great. And?"

Omar took a deep breath, preparing himself to speak the words. "I just never planned on falling in love. With anyone. I wanted it to be Anahita and that was it. It doesn't seem fair to her to move on."

"To...Anahita?" Zahir creased his brow.

Omar nodded. "Why should I move on if she can't?"

Zahir blinked, studying him. "But you've been out with women..."

"One-night stands," Omar said, waving his hand in the air. "That's all. They don't mean anything."

"But Marian does."

Omar nodded glumly, reaching for his tumbler. "Yeah. She does."

Zahir tapped his glass, narrowing his eyes. "I thought you were the problem solver of the family."

"This is one problem I can't figure out," Omar said, taking a sip of his drink. "I'm too close to it. All I know is that when I'm around Marian, I feel great. But then the guilt comes crashing down, and I want to die. Because I know that by all rights, I should still be with Anahita, and we'd have children by now, and I wouldn't even take a second look at Marian."

"But that's not what life is, brother," Zahir said, placing a hand on his shoulder. Omar deflated a little. "That's not how it turned out."

"So what am I supposed to do?"

"Confront what life is giving you." Zahir slapped him on the shoulder. "You're living in the past. It's time to move on. Anahita would have wanted that."

"She wanted to be alive and to be with me," Omar said softly. "She wouldn't have wanted me to be with someone else."

His words lingered in the air, drifting strangely between them. They sounded absurd as he thought about them, but this was the personal hell he'd created for himself since her death.

"Obviously, being with you was the first plan." Zahir's voice was soft, compassionate. "But you can't be married to a ghost. You can't build a life with someone who isn't here. She never wanted you to suffer for the rest of your life. But the more important question is what do *you* want, in the life you're living now?"

Omar rubbed at his face. Zahir made sense—these were the words he'd needed to hear for too long. Far too long.

"I never realized you felt this way, brother," Zahir said, squeezing his shoulder. "I just thought you had…moved on."

Omar swallowed a knot in his throat. It didn't help that he tortured himself with his wife's memory by keeping her pictures all over the house and rereading her letters to him regularly. *Maybe you should stop doing those things.*

"Yeah, well, I guess I just wanted everyone to think I was fine." Omar squeezed his hands together, as if it might relieve some of the pressure inside him. And even now, in the midst of mourning Anahita, he craved Marian. So badly that he almost didn't know how to handle it.

He'd ignored her texts from earlier that evening. He had to, for his own sanity. He couldn't be trusted to respond or talk to her until he got his head straight. But Zahir had screwed it back into place just enough.

"I can't imagine what that must have been like," Zahir said. "We all grieved when she passed. But you were the closest of anyone."

Omar nodded, studying the far wall, his gaze sliding over the sculpture she'd picked out just weeks after they'd married, a ballet dancer in bronze. He opened his mouth to speak but was interrupted by a knock on his door.

Omar stiffened, casting a curious glance at Zahir. Unexpected knocks were few and far between. It had to be one of the family, but he wasn't expecting Imaad at this hour.

"I'll get it," Omar said, furrowing a brow. He hopped to his feet, the rugs leading to the front door soft under his bare feet. As he pulled the door open, he bit back a gasp. Marian stood in the doorway, looking timid and nervous.

"Hey." She waved a little, brushing back her curls.

Omar blinked at her. Maybe his conversation with Zahir had produced her out of thin air, or called to her like a snake charmer. "What are you doing here?"

"We need to talk."

He squinted. Maybe this was a dream. "How do you even know where I live?"

Her mouth fell open, like maybe she was having second thoughts. "I—I asked Annabelle. She told me. I hope it isn't a prob—"

"And who let you up?" The incredulity swirled inside of him. This seemed like a blessing in disguise.

"The doorman! And then that lady at the desk, the one with the gray hair; she said her name but it was long and complicated." Marian winced. "I'm sorry, I know it's Sunday and it's late, but I really need to talk to you."

Omar blinked at her, pulling open the door. He wanted to wrap his arms around her, press those curves against him. A day apart felt like a year. "Come in."

Marian stepped inside hesitantly, looking around like his apartment was a museum after-hours. Zahir rose from the couch, nodding her way.

"Oh, hi." Marian tucked her hair behind an ear. "I didn't mean to interrupt. This is actually business-related."

Zahir smiled professionally, setting his tumbler on the coffee table as he came toward the door. "No worries. I was just on my way out, actually." He squeezed Omar's shoulder and then clasped Marian's hand in his. "It was a pleasure to see you, Marian. Have a good night."

Zahir let himself out and shut the door behind him quietly, as though to not disturb the scene he was leaving. Omar shook his head a little, like the motion might jostle him back into clarity.

"Sorry, Marian, I—" He pinched the bridge of his nose, gesturing toward the couch. "Have a seat. I wasn't expecting you."

"I know, I know. I texted, and I called. But when you didn't answer, I decided to just swing by and see you. Desperate measures, Omar. I swear." She collapsed onto the couch, sighing dramatically.

Omar paused beside her. "Do you want a drink?"

She looked at the half-full tumbler of whiskey Zahir had left. "What was he drinking?"

"Whiskey."

She took the glass and gulped back the rest of it, which made Omar smile. Every damn thing she did was great. "That's fine. I might get another one soon. Listen, we need to talk."

Omar nodded and eased down onto the couch next to her. His gaze careened up and down her body. She'd opted for simple leggings and a loose top, but even that made him desperate to smooth his hands underneath the fabric, retrace those curves he'd denied himself the night before.

"I'm sorry I didn't respond. I was with family," he said simply.

"It's okay. I figured you would assume it was…personal. Which, trust me, this isn't." She shook her head, eyes wide. "I found out something else from my girl in New York."

Omar nodded, his eyes soldered to the fascinating arc of her shoulder peeking out from her top. "What is it?"

"National Oil had an altercation with someone we know," she said, rooting him to his seat with her gaze. "Kelly Gunther."

The words made a few rounds in his head before they really sank in. He furrowed a brow. "What did you say?"

"She found out that he never made his way back to the US as he should have. Kelly went to National Oil for some reason, and it ended with his arrest."

Omar stared at her, desperate to not believe it. "Oh God. That seems…impossible."

"My girl knows her sources. And I'm sure we can both guess his goal in going to National Oil."

Omar groaned into his hands, leaning back against the couch. "Hell. This is why they never called on Friday. It has to be."

"I thought this required immediate action," Marian said, reaching for the tumbler again. "Where can I fill this up?"

Omar started to point out the bar then stood up and offered to do it himself. He wanted another one now, too. "I think we can send an email to start."

"And request a phone conference, at least, sometime tomorrow."

"Exactly." Omar filled her glass, and then his own. He returned to the couch, handing her the tumbler. She took a gulp.

"I don't think he'd get too far with leaking information. Not with how rude and horrible he is," Marian said, wincing against the alcohol. "My main worry is he's ruined our good name."

Omar shook his head, sipping tersely at his drink. "And we should be prepared if he has." He came to his feet, heading for his briefcase by the front door. "A little preemptive planning is in order."

CHAPTER THIRTEEN

Marian yawned and rubbed at her eyes. After two solid hours of diagramming every potential secret or foible that Kelly could use against them and their diplomatic responses, the looming crisis felt more like an eventual blip. Kelly might try to take them down, but he wouldn't. His revenge attempt would prove ineffective.

"I think this is good," Omar said, pushing away the papers they'd been working on at his elegant dining room table. Everything in his penthouse looked like it came from an interior design magazine. Was that his or his wife's touch? She was afraid to ask.

"Yeah. Good enough, at least." Marian picked up her empty tumbler, heading for the sink in the adjacent kitchen. She set it on the counter, furtively sizing up the arrangement of the room. Marble countertops, bereft of utensils and appliances. Everything gleamed and sparkled. Omar was so *neat*.

She turned and inhaled sharply when she found Omar in the doorway, his arm propped against the molding. His dark eyes gobbled her up in a very specific non-business way, but this was where the real test began: standing her ground.

"You have a lovely kitchen," she said, breezing past him, trying to ignore the heat that rolled off his body. She headed for the living room, where she'd left her shoes. "I'll get out of your hair now. It's getting late."

Congratulations. You did it. She lamely patted herself on the back in her head while she slipped her flats on. Now you can go home and masturbate while thinking about Omar.

She noticed her phone on the dining room table where they'd been planning, so she diverted, her footsteps making a soft *snick-snick* against the smooth wood floor. Omar stood at the far end of the table, his jaw flexing as he watched her. The silence sizzled between them.

"Just need this," she said as she grabbed her phone, her voice withering in the tension between them. *God, what is this?* She tried to force a little laugh, but it stuck in her throat. Omar's eyes were like obsidian.

"Okay, well," she said, turning for the door. Just get out the door. Unless he asks you to stay. Please ask me to stay. I have so little time left here.

But no. She would do well to reaffirm the professional boundaries. She already knew what the romantic entanglements would bring with Omar—more conflict and confusion about his past. And she didn't have time for that. She couldn't heal him when he was clearly still so hurt.

"Marian, stay with me."

His gruff words made her freeze in her spot. She stared at the door, hesitant to turn around. Thoughts raced in her head, but nothing seemed clear or right. Staying the night was all she wanted to do. But she would only want more, and more. And Omar could never give her that. For his own reasons, but also for practical reasons.

She spun slowly on her heel, daring to meet his gaze. He approached slowly, his request still echoing in the air between them.

"I don't know if I should." She swallowed hard, looking around. This beautiful penthouse palace, where he'd lived with his wife. Her being here reeked of a bad idea. *You'll regret this if you stay. When he pulls away. When he makes this awkward. When he grows cold.*

"I know that you should," Omar said, reaching out to touch her arm. The small caress blasted through her, made her knees weak. *Damn you, Omar.*

"Trust me, I want to—" she began.

"Then do it."

Her words shriveled in her throat. "But I think you might be better off if we don't do this anymore." She gestured to the air between them. "You know?"

"No." Omar took one more step to close the gap between them and slid his hand around the back of her neck, pressing his mouth against hers. A slow, thorough, exploratory kiss wiped away every contrary thought from her brain.

"Okay," she gasped when the kiss broke. "Okay, yeah, I'll stay."

Omar grinned boyishly, pulling her by the hand toward the hallway. "Come. We should go to bed."

She stumbled after him, a haze settling over her. This felt right—*too* right—but the logical side of her still whispered to keep her distance. Like that was possible anymore. Omar pushed her by the hips into his bedroom, his eyes ablaze as he followed her like a predator.

"Lovely bedroom," Marian said, barely glancing around. All she caught was dark gray bedcovers and starkly framed black-and-white photos.

"Mm-hmm." Omar pinned her to the bed and she fell backwards, a giggle escaping her. He climbed on top of her, showering her face with a flurry of kisses. She clutched at his head, welcoming everything, desperate for this sensation to never end.

God, if only you lived in New York...

She pushed the thought away, along with a slew of other things that ensured this would never work out long-term. And why was she even thinking long-term anyway? Why couldn't this just be a harmless Parsian fling?

Omar flipped her over onto her belly and tugged at her leggings, bringing them down to her knees. He took a bite of each ass cheek, his fingers slipping beneath the damp fabric of her panties.

"Ooooh." Marian let out a low moan as his fingers went straight for the sweet spot. He knocked and prodded at her clit, prompting dizzying waves of satisfaction. Their one day apart had felt interminable; they had so much to catch up on now.

"I love these pants you wore," he whispered hotly into her ear. The weight of him pressed against her was too delicious to bear. "They turned me on immediately."

"Some people don't consider them pants," she breathed, rubbing her butt against the hard line of his cock. "They're just leggings."

"Well, whatever they are…I vote you wear them to the office every day."

Something about his words sent happiness spiraling through her. Even the briefest hint at a future warmed her. *Damn you, Omar!* He leaned back for a moment to step out of his pants and briefs. Then he nuzzled her ass cheeks, tugging her panties down to join her leggings.

"I want every part of you," he growled, nuzzling her legs apart. She gasped as his tongue traced the lips of her pussy, passing gently over her clit. He slurped and suckled from behind, an interesting angle that stoked her fire more intensely than normal. She moaned and writhed against the bed, knotting the covers in her hand.

Omar sighed softly, then nestled his cock in between her legs. She arched up to meet him and he pressed himself inside slowly, a low groan escaping him as he did. She moaned along with him, suddenly so grateful for his heat and the fullness that tears pricked at her eyes. Jesus, this man made her think crazy things. Nobody had ever felt so good with her, or inside her.

"Marian." Omar grabbed an ass cheek in his hand so hard that it hurt. She bucked against him, and he started a slow rhythm, one that brought her to the precipice in record time. He snaked a hand underneath her shirt, seeking a breast, cupping it gently.

They moved together in jerky unison, desperate pants escaping them, the friction leading to a delicious climax.

"I'm close, Omar," she whispered, pinching her eyes shut. She fisted the bedspread as she took another long, deep thrust from him, which made her breasts jiggle.

He pounded into her, gripping at her hips to hold her in place. He thrust again and again, until Marian's pussy clenched and the freefall was impossible to ignore. Her orgasm spilled over and consumed her, but he didn't relent, slamming into her with long, frenzied thrusts that pushed her to new heights each time. She let out a wail, something throaty and foreign, as the pleasure wracked her over and over.

Omar groaned a moment later and slowed his movements, stilling as he pulsed hot inside her. His chest heaved as he collapsed onto her. Her eyes drifted open and shut as the powerful climax receded into a pleasant buzz.

"Holy...hell." Her voice came out weak and muffled.

"Mmmm." His cock throbbed inside her. A moment later he slipped out and fell onto the bed next to her, cupping her face in his hand.

She snuggled up to his smooth chest. Three little words hung heavy on her tongue, but she wouldn't say them. It didn't seem right to say them. Not now, probably not ever. But they were there, despite all the logic and rationale in the world.

They smiled lazily at one another until sleep overcame her and she drifted off.

*　　*　　*

Hours later, Marian awoke with a start. Bladder aching, she fumbled around for a moment, trying to get her bearings. She was still at Omar's, but where again? She squinted in the darkness, trying to make out anything familiar. A bedside clock glowed with an ungodly hour: 3:21 a.m. She swallowed a dry taste in her mouth and swung her legs over the bed. Omar must have tucked her in, since she was magically covered with sheets and a blanket. He must have taken her shirt off, too, because she was definitely nude.

She smiled as she stumbled out of the bedroom, unsure where the bathroom might be. There had to be one close to his room. She glanced both ways down the hall; to the left was the living room, and to the right were a slew of closed doors. It had to be one of those.

She grabbed at the handle of the first room, flipping on the light. A spare bedroom. She turned off the light and shut the door, trying the next one. A closet. She grunted, trying the next one in line. His office.

His scent hung in the air, drawing her inside. The light she flipped on glowed soft yellow, illuminating his bookcases and a wide, spacious desk. She blinked as she took it in. Just a quick glance, like being a tourist.

She walked along the bookcase, checking out the spines she could read in English. She grinned. Some detective novels, Plato, and plenty of cookbooks. A diverse selection. She dragged a finger over his desktop, needing just a few more glimpses before she left, despite her straining bladder. A notebook sat open on his desk, papers splayed out. She peered down at the writing, something elegant and feminine staring up at her.

My dearest Omar…it's impossible to describe how much I've come to love you! It's like years have passed instead of months. I know that once I pass on, I'll continue loving you for eternity. Yours forever, Anahita

Marian blinked, rereading the short letter. There were stacks of them. Each one on a piece of stationery. She'd spent her days writing letters to Omar. She flipped through them—most were in Farsi, but a couple stood out in English. She read as much as she could until she heard something in the distance. And whatever it was, she wouldn't risk being caught in his office. She hurried out of the room, clicking the light off and the door shut.

The next room she tried was the bathroom, a huge, white arena with a jacuzzi tub and two sinks. She stared at the white tiles as she peed, the love letters heavy on her mind.

What was she doing here, when she knew this was a bad idea? Clearly he'd read them recently, if they were sitting out on his otherwise clear desk like that. He probably read them every night before he went to bed, for two full years. She rubbed at her face, the truth settling into her.

She'd stepped into something she should have never gotten mixed up with. Just do the job and leave—that was her only mission. And it was time to stick to the plan.

Marian returned to the bedroom, tiptoeing quietly around the room as she searched for her clothes in the darkness. Omar snored softly as she dressed once she found all of her clothes folded neatly on a chair in the corner. Things like that made her smile…things like that she'd miss about Omar.

But this would never work.

CHAPTER FOURTEEN

Omar readied for work the next morning feeling lost. Finding out Marian had left in the night rubbed him the wrong way. Why would she do that? He scowled at his reflection as he adjusted his tie in the bathroom mirror. They'd had a lovely evening, even fallen asleep together.

It's because of Anahita.

He still hadn't addressed that looming issue, but how? He needed to come clean to her, to admit that maybe he was ready to try for something new but also maybe he would never love again. Though maybe he already loved Marian. Confusion shuddered through him. None of this made sense. And the longer it didn't make sense, the more he would push Marian away.

On his way to the office, a text came in from Marian. "I'll be working from the hotel today. Not feeling well."

He tapped a quick response. "Is that why you left in the middle of the night?"

Her reply text took a few moments too long. *"Yeah. Sorry. Didn't want to wake you."*

"I hope you feel better…is there anything I can do?"

Her reply this time came lightning fast. *"No thanks."*

He frowned at his phone, pocketing it before heading downstairs to meet the car. He felt all jumbled and unstable on the inside, and he hated that feeling. He needed equilibrium, and fast. At the office, Omar jumped into the swing of things quickly, eager to lose himself in the day's tasks.

His first order of business was calling National Oil about the pending deal. Armed with the document that he and Marian had brainstormed the night before, he was put through to their CEO. Omar made a quick speech about why they should meet and discuss any potential repercussions of Kelly Gunther's unexpected visit. Surprisingly, the CEO suggested he come around to Almasi Holdings for a one-on-one meeting.

"I'll have my colleague join us then," Omar said on his desk phone as he reached for his cell phone. Marian needed to be here. "She's away from the office now, but I'm sure she can—"

"No, just the two of us will be fine. After all this commotion with the American man…I want to do things more traditionally." The CEO's tone left no room for discussion. And of course it had to do with Marian being female. Omar had known from the start that these men wouldn't like working with a woman. Now Kelly's ruckus had given them the excuse they needed to edge Marian out of the picture. "See you in a half hour."

Omar set the phone down gently, wondering what had prompted such an immediate interest in sealing the deal. He blinked at his cellphone, indecision gnawing at him. This would be easier if Marian had come into the office. Between her not feeling well and the CEO's demand, maybe it would be best to just see him and finish it up.

That was what they both wanted, after all.

But this was *their* deal. Finishing it without her seemed wrong. He blew a puff of air between his lips, struggling to make the wisest decision. Who was it more important to please in this case: the gatekeeper for the deal or a colleague?

He checked his watch. Time was ticking. He tapped out a quick message to Marian. *"Will you come in at all today?"*

As he waited for a response, he knew exactly what his father would say: seal the deal. The business comes first.

And as time wore on and Marian didn't respond, it seemed his decision was made for him.

He tapped on his desk, waiting for the National Oil CEO to show up.

* * *

Three hours later, Omar had a signed agreement in his hands, freshly penned by both him and the CEO of National Oil. The best possible outcome that both he and Marian had envisioned— good equipment, transparency in stakeholders, and no more nonsense coming from Kelly Gunther, who was apparently back on a flight to the US. He couldn't wait to tell Marian.

But first, lunch. He texted Marian to see if she'd join him, but all he got was a *"No thanks."* This news had to be shared in person, or she might take it wrong. Face-to-face was the only way.

After a quick lunch at his favorite café down the street, he returned to his office humming. He loosened his tie as he settled into his seat, ready to tackle emails and correspondence for the rest of his afternoon. The major headache of the week was out of the way. Smooth sailing from here.

He worked quietly for a long while, the only sounds the distant honking of the traffic six stories below. He tensed when he heard stomping in the hallway, followed by his doorknob turning.

The door swung open, and Marian stormed in, her eyes on fire.

"What the fuck did you do this morning?" She strode up to his desk and cocked a hip, arms crossed over her chest. Anger sizzled in the air around her. He gaped up at her, unsure how he could respond and keep his life intact.

"What's going on?"

"You sealed the deal *without me*," she spat, leaning over his desk. "What the fuck do you think you're doing?"

He leaned back in his chair, holding up a hand. "Listen—"

"No, I will not listen to you. I got an email from Mr. Thomas lauding your exceptional deal-making skills. Did he mention me even once, or all the hard work I put in? No. Of fucking course not. So why am I even surprised that you ran off with all my brainstorming and made this deal behind my back?"

"That is *not* how it went down," he began.

"Oh, really? Well, it looks to me like you met with the CEO this morning and signed the deal without me. Or did it go some other way?" She leaned closer, cocking a brow.

Omar swallowed hard, formulating the most diplomatic response possible. He'd never seen her angry before—this was like reasoning with a bull. "The CEO contacted me last-minute for a meeting. He showed up so fast that I didn't have time to get you involved. Besides, he asked for a private—"

"Bullshit. Pure. Bullshit." She laughed scornfully. "You'd think that at the *very least* you could have included me in the paperwork or made some mention to *my boss* that I had any hand in this success." She shook her head, mouth tugged down into an angry frown.

Omar held her gaze, no matter how much it stung. "I'm sorry." He hadn't even known that his father had shared the good news with Mr. Thomas already. It seemed like a cruel joke. But Marian was in no mood to hear his side.

"Well, I guess this means I can just go home now. You got what you wanted—the deal and a quick lay." She spun, slamming the door shut behind her as she stormed out.

Omar let his head fall to his hands, her words spinning inside him like a tornado. He grimaced as the pain washed through him over and over again. Her parting shot wasn't anywhere near the truth. That wasn't what he'd wanted from her.

Omar clutched at his head as a headache throbbed to life, and he struggled to figure out the best next step. He couldn't let Marian think that he had planned this betrayal. If anything, he needed to tell her just what he felt for her…and what he was prepared to attempt with her.

He reached for his phone, dialed her number. It rang once before it clicked over to voicemail, so he tried again. Same result. She was most likely ignoring his calls.

He groaned, tossing the phone on the desk. Nothing felt good or right anymore. And there was only one clear desire: to have Marian back at his side.

CHAPTER FIFTEEN

Marian fumed in the taxi to the hotel as she searched for last-minute flights on her phone. She'd be returning to NYC that evening, come hell or high water. She was sure Mr. Thomas wouldn't mind, since in his eyes she'd been merely an accessory to the deal.

As she searched, Mr. Thomas called. She answered, trying to hide the hurt in her voice. "Hello?"

"There you are. So, are you preparing for your return?"

"Yes, I'm looking for flights now." She swallowed a knot in her throat, looking out the window as the sights of Minarak breezed by.

"I'm glad to hear negotiations are finished. Very pleased to see that email from Mr. Almasi." Mr. Thomas cleared his throat. "But why weren't you mentioned?"

She pinched her eyes shut. "I assure you sir, I was there. I was at every meeting, save for today's." She swallowed a surge of anger. "Omar can vouch that I was there every step of the way." *And if he doesn't, then he deserves to have his balls removed.*

Mr. Thomas harrumphed from across the world. "Well, I'm sure you did a fine job. Kept everything organized, as you always do."

Her heart sank. She'd done more than a fine organization job. She'd carried this deal…and received none of the glory. "Of course."

Back at the hotel, she purchased the earliest flight possible and packed as quickly as she could. *Peace, Parsabad.* She'd be back in NYC by the following day, and it couldn't be soon enough. In just under an hour, she was airport-ready. She breezed out of the room and down into the reception area, leaving her key at the front desk.

During the ride to the airport, she wavered between torturous memories of Omar's sweet kisses and recalling Annabelle's story about being detained in the name of love. Or so the story went, now that Annabelle and Imaad told it as if it were legend. How he had security hold her up at the airport so he could offer his private jet, to get her back to her sick mother sooner.

She smiled sadly. Her story with the Almasi middle brother had turned out significantly different. Though deep down, a part of her was desperate for that romantic gesture. Maybe he'd be waiting at the airport—or maybe he'd already called the guards to refuse her passport.

You're thinking like a crazy woman. Yet it was hard not to be hopeful. She wanted so badly to be wrong about him. But her own parting words cycled like a tornado in her mind. He'd used her for a business deal and for sex, while all along she'd thought him to be an equal, even potential partner material.

It was the greatest let-down of her life. No, worse. The greatest embarrassment of her life. She'd failed on the romantic front *and* the professional front, all in one blazing downfall.

Check-in at the airport went smoothly, since she was about five hours early. Nobody stopped her through security, and the longer she waited in front of gate B27, the more convinced she became that her disappearance from Parsabad would likely not even register with Omar.

She'd been a blip, when she'd thought it was a boom.

*   *   *

After one excruciatingly long direct flight to New York City, Marian stumbled through the JFK airport like a zombie, unsure if it was very early Parsian time or super-late NYC time. She wobbled as she went through customs, the week and a half away from home feeling more like a full month. The vowels and consonants of her fellow Americans rang strangely between her ears. She rolled her luggage glumly through the baggage claim and picked up the first taxi she could. *Home sweet home.*

The low point came when she got back to her studio apartment in Brooklyn. Just before pushing open the door, she stilled herself, wondering if maybe Omar was waiting for her on the other side. *How would that even be possible?* She pushed it open, finding a dark, stale apartment waiting for her. No Omar. Not even junk mail under the door.

Was she that desperate to hear from him? Not even a peep since she'd left his office the afternoon before. And now, halfway across the world, even yesterday in Parsabad felt like a distant fantasy. One that she was unable to even fathom from within the confines of Brooklyn.

Marian quickly fell asleep, back in her own bed. Strange dreams plagued her, but when she awoke around nine the next morning, she felt refreshed and ready to tackle the day. Back in the swing of things in New York. Exactly like before. *Pre-Omar.*

She shuddered. There'd be none of those thoughts now that she was back. She needed to banish him from her mind. Even though part of her wilted on the inside at the concept. They'd been so good together. And he'd been so sweet. How had things ended this way? Why had he done that to her?

The confusion irritated her almost as much as the lack of caffeine. She called Layla for an impromptu welcome-home coffee date on her self-declared transition day. She needed a day to decompress, buy groceries, and take excessive naps before heading back to the office the next morning. They met at their favorite spot in Brooklyn, just ten minutes from Marian's building.

"It's so good to see you!" Layla wrapped her in a tight hug, her sparkling strawberry blonde hair smelling of flowers, as always. Marian sighed into her friend's embrace, grateful for the familiar contact.

"God, it's good to be back." Marian collapsed into a wrought iron chair on the back patio of the coffee shop, thankful for the bright sun and light breeze. A waitress came for their order and they got what they always did—two red eye coffees.

"So tell me. How did the deal go?"

Marian leveled her with a look. "It went. But not so well, for me."

"Oh no." Concern creased Layla's face. "What happened?"

Marian gave her the CliffsNotes version of how Omar had sealed the deal without her, making her own boss think she'd had little to do with the success.

"That doesn't make sense," Layla said. "You two were so good together. You worked so well, I thought."

"Yeah, I thought so too." Marian scoffed. "He hasn't even called or anything since I left, so I guess that's my answer. It was just a fling for business purposes." She scoffed. "And the worst part is, I really thought we had...*something* between us. You know? Like, I felt that spark. And I thought he did too."

Layla frowned as the waitress set down their coffees, her eyes on the table. "Some guys just aren't…ready, I guess."

"Yeah, and he was the least ready of all." Marian shook her head, stirring a spoonful of sugar into her mug. "I should have known from the start that I could never compete with his dead wife."

Layla grimaced. "Was it that bad?"

"Jesus, it was practically a chastity belt!" She paused, sipping at her coffee. "That's a lie. If he tried to be chaste, he failed. Miserably. We couldn't stop having sex."

Layla squeezed her arm. "Was it at least good?"

"Ugh. The best." Marian crumpled into her seat, memories flooding her. "That's the thing. Everything seemed so good. Like, within three days, I was already thinking about a future with this man."

Layla widened her eyes. "Wow."

"Yeah. Except, not wow. Major letdown, in fact." Marian sighed tersely, the cup of coffee steaming in front of her lips. "I dunno. I'll get over it. Or maybe I won't."

Layla pouted. "Honey, you will. I promise you. You're made of steel. You'll bounce back."

"Maybe I'm tired of bouncing back." She took a contemplative sip of her coffee, sullenness making her limbs heavy. "Maybe I just want to not fall over and over again and have no one there to pick me up but myself."

"But you're stronger for it, honey."

"I dunno." Marian felt a dark cloud overcoming her. "Because now, at work, I'll have to work even harder to prove to my boss that I even do anything. He thinks I just took notes and kept everyone on track, but I carried a solid half of the deal. All I can do is go back to work and keep hoping for another opportunity to arise. But if I stay there, I might run into Omar again. And how horrible would that be? It might be better if I just quit."

Layla let out a low breath. "Wow. You sure about all that?"

"No. But that's how it's looking right now."

"Listen, girl, you need to finish that coffee before you make any rash decisions. And then just go to work tomorrow and see what happens. I'm sure this isn't as bad as you think. And really…I think you just have a broken heart."

Marian frowned. "Yeah. Stupid dumb heartbreaking guys from Parsabad."

Layla wrapped her in a hug. "It'll get easier with time. And until it does, I'll take you out to forget." She kissed the top of her head, and then clinked her mug against hers. "Partying helps everything."

CHAPTER SIXTEEN

Omar spent a restless evening in his penthouse after Marian's outburst. His throat was tight, and he couldn't get a full breath of air, no matter how deeply he breathed. His game plan was to give her space and go over to her hotel after dinner.

But around eight p.m., he got the news from Annabelle—Marian had flown home.

The revelation crushed him, made him both dizzy and exhausted at the same time. He reached for his phone to call her, but again it clicked straight to voicemail. Of course it would—she was hundreds of miles up in the air. He didn't leave a message, choosing instead to pace his living room while he concocted a plan.

What now? He certainly couldn't leave things in the state they were now. If only to get his side heard, to let Marian know the truth, to have her not *hate him*. But if things really went his way, he'd have a chance to tell her how he felt. That she was more than just a special woman—she was the only woman he'd ever felt tempted to try anything with. Since before Anahita even.

One thing he would do now. He hurried into his office, finding the familiar book of love letters scattered across his desk. He reread them occasionally and had done so more often during

Marian's stay. He'd turned to them as a guide, but they'd led him into a thicket. He had to get rid of them.

It was time to end the chapter.

He settled into his desk chair, spreading the letters out one last time, just as he'd done so many times over the past two years. He studied each one carefully, appreciating for the last time the curls of her Farsi, the angles of her English, the poetic way she had of writing to him, even while laid up in bed during his work days. The letters served as a sort of journal of their quickly arcing relationship, one that started as strangers but ended as heartfelt lovers.

But that story was over. It had been over for a long time. And he could not deny his emotions, especially his feelings for Marian. Not for Anahita, not for anyone else. It was simply impossible.

Omar read each letter for the last time, smiling at her musings, laughing at some of her observations about his brothers or the hospital staff. And when he'd combed through everything, he scooped them all into a pile and carried them into the living room.

He pressed the electric starter for the gas fireplace, watching as the controlled fire leapt to life. And then, one by one, he tossed the letters into the hungry orange flames, watching as each one was swallowed up into a black abyss in the heart of the flame. He fed the fire until he had no more to feed it, and then he sat for a long time watching the paper disintegrate into ash.

It was almost eleven p.m. when he snapped out of it, and he immediately called his father.

His father's groggy voice answered. "Hello?"

"Sorry for the late call," Omar said, feeling suddenly breathless. "But I have to go to America."

There was a long pause on the other end of the line. "For what?"

"Marian."

His father sighed. "What?"

"Will you support my decision?" His throat tightened. He'd go whether or not he had his father's blessing, but it would be nice to have it. "I've fallen in love with her. I want to be with her. And she left the country thinking I'd used her. I have to go make it right."

There was a soft chuckle from his father. "You boys never cease to amaze me."

Omar relaxed a little. "This is just something that I have to do."

"I'm happy to see that you've healed," his father said. "Go to her. We'll make sure everything is covered at the office."

Omar hung up the phone, his entire body buoyant with excitement. This just didn't feel necessary, this felt more right than anything he'd ever done. He texted Annabelle to see if she was still up, and she called almost immediately.

"Is everything okay?" Her voice sounded strained.

"It will be," Omar said. "I need your help. I want to fly to New York to surprise Marian, but I need some information first."

Annabelle hummed appreciatively. "Do I smell a grand gesture in the works?"

"Not as good as being a border detainee, but we can't all work at Imaad's level," Omar cracked. "We parted on bad—well, horrible—terms. I have to go make it right. And I don't think I can survive without her, honestly."

Annabelle cackled. "Oh, God. Like I didn't see this coming from a mile away."

Omar grinned despite the anxiety gnawing him alive. So many things had yet to fall into place. Every second, his plan coalesced more inside his head.

"This has to be a surprise. But I need her address and contact information for someone who can help me over there."

"The first one is easy. And the second is…" Annabelle paused, and then squealed. "I know who it is! Layla! One of her closest friends in NYC. I can send you her information as soon as we hang up."

"Great." Relief flooded him, and a to-do list began materializing in his head. "And Annabelle, I just want you to know, I didn't sell her out, or throw her under the bus, or use her for anything." He swallowed hard. "I'm just crazy about her."

"Awww, Omar." Annabelle tutted. "Pack your shit and go find her!"

When he hung up the phone, he felt energized and ready to tackle everything. He'd arrange his departure on the family jet for first thing in the morning, meaning he'd get to NYC sometime in the morning their time. And hopefully along the way, he'd be able to solidify the final details with Layla about the surprise plan percolating in his head.

Glancing one last time at the glowing embers in the fireplace, he realized that small gesture had freed him in a way he hadn't counted on.

Freed him up for an entirely new future with Marian.

CHAPTER SEVENTEEN

Layla texted incessantly about going out that night. All through her first day back in the office, Marian could barely keep up with the pinging messages about outfit choices and makeup looks. Layla always had a penchant for date nights, but this seemed excessive. Maybe she was taking Marian's sadness and making it her own.

"Damn girl, calm down. I might not want to go out tonight. Let's see how work goes," Marian responded to a string of 13 texts.

"WE ARE GOING OUT TONIGHT NO QUESTIONS," Layla responded.

Marian frowned at the phone screen. Well, that was settled. She turned to her computer, finishing the email she'd started. Half a day back in her regular spot in the regular office and already it seemed a little bland. Like maybe nothing had changed in her absence…and maybe that nothing ever would change.

She'd relished the freedom and agency of her temporary position abroad. Having that sort of negotiation power and importance was a welcome change. Far better than being an executive assistant, even though she was paid handsomely and loved her job.

She was ready for more. And as far as she could see, her next chance for more might never come.

She sighed heavily, returning to the email. Work today was a struggle. Between Layla's texts and wondering about Omar, she was about braindead. And still no word from him, which only convinced her further that he'd entirely forgotten about her and moved on. Her disappearance probably just made it so easy for him, fit perfectly into his stupid little plan. She scoffed.

Layla texted again. "I think you should wear that green dress, the one with the scoop back."

Marian picked up her phone in a huff. "We're not going to the MET, Layla. We're going to a BAR. Why do I have to get so fancy?"

"I want to go to a fancy place before the bar, I thought I told you. Aren't you reading my messages??"

Marian scrolled up, finding a brief mention of a fancy place. "Sorry. Ok fine, fancy dress. Whatever. You dress me. I don't even care, I just want fucking martinis."

Layla sent a smiley face, and Marian watched her phone a moment longer, just to be sure no other queries were coming. When it seemed Layla the Dress Code Goddess had been appeased, Marian returned to her work.

She made it ten minutes before Layla texted again. *"I'll be over at 5:30 to start getting ready."*

Marian's eyes widened. What did she think this was, Saturday night? It was a *Wednesday*. She shook her head. Incredible. She'd have to leave work exactly on time to make it home before Layla got there.

Marian made it through the rest of her workday somehow and then squeaked out of work just a few minutes early to get a head start on the commute to Brooklyn. As predicted, Layla was waiting in the hallway with a backpack when Marian arrived, smiling like she knew a secret.

"It's a night to celebrate," Layla said, following Marian inside the apartment.

"What are we celebrating? The fact that I'm still single?" Marian dropped her purse on the counter.

"No. Well, only if you want to, but that seems a little sad. We should rephrase it, at any rate. I would like to celebrate the fact that I'm quitting my job."

Marian turned slowed to her friend, eyes wide. "Really?"

Layla grinned, nodding excitedly. "Yep! I finally made the decision."

"So this means you'll come work with us, right?" Marian winked at her.

Layla laughed, but it died off quickly. "No, actually, I'm going to travel for a while. I have enough savings to last me at least a year and a half, maybe two, if I play my cards right. I'll have to get a job again eventually, but, damn…I'm ready." She blew a puff of air from her mouth. "I put in my two weeks today."

Marian squealed. "Wow! That's so exciting! Congratulations!" The two friends hopped around. "Now I see why you're so hellbent on getting out tonight!'"

Layla smiled mysteriously and scooted into the bathroom. "I'm going to start getting ready!"

Marian cleaned up the kitchen before heading to her dresser to pull out the appropriate necessities: sheer stockings and a push-up bra. She stripped out of her work clothes and shimmied into the tights and bra just as Layla came out of the bathroom in a form-fitting blue dress.

"That's cute," Marian remarked. "Totally good for an 'I'm quitting my job' night out on the town."

Layla grabbed her make-up bag and stood in front of the full-length mirror on the far wall. "Thanks. I thought so, too."

The two friends readied relatively quickly amid pop music and a few anecdotes about Marian's trip to Parsabad. By the time six thirty rolled around, the two were smoking hot and ready to go.

"This feels great already," Marian said, locking the apartment door behind her. They strutted down the hallway like bad bitches and then hailed a cab like they owned the world.

In the taxi on the way to their first stop, Layla was bubbling. "This is gonna be such a great night. You'll see that not all men are bad. There are some good ones out there."

Marian lifted a perfectly painted brow. "I thought this was about your upcoming travels."

"Well, yeah, that too." Layla patted at her hair, stealing a glimpse in the rear-view mirror. "But this is also about you feeling good. Feeling *better*."

Marian shrugged. "Whatever it is, we look awesome, and there's gonna be vodka."

Layla grinned. "Exactly."

About fifteen minutes later the taxi pulled up to their destination, a Mediterranean restaurant Marian had never heard of. A car horn blared behind them as they approached the main doors, and the smattering of people on the sidewalk stared at them.

Inside, the restaurant was strangely empty. Not a single patron filled any table, despite the entre place being illuminated.

"Whoa," Marian muttered.

"We must be early," Layla said. "I made a reservation, even. Looks like we didn't need it." She laughed a little as the maître d' led them to a table with banquettes in the far corner of the restaurant. The two sat down, receiving stiff board menus, and a moment later, a waiter appeared with water and a bottle of wine.

"Compliments of the house," he said, bowing slightly as he poured the wine.

"Was this a Groupon or something?" Marian whispered.

"I have to go to the bathroom," Layla blurted, jolting to her feet. "I'll be back." Layla trotted off into the recesses of the restaurant. When she disappeared around a corner, Marian stared peering around. Something seemed off, but she didn't know what. The disturbing lack of people irked her. Maybe she just wanted to be ogled, and since there was no crowd, it was a letdown.

I wish Omar could see me now. She'd love to send him a selfie of herself in this hot dress, all dolled up, let him see what he was missing. She smiled smugly. If only she'd allow herself to message him. But maybe after a few martinis, she'd break down. Probably she'd drunk-confess to him that she *loved* him. The word hung bulky and threatening in the back of her mind. Just a little loosening of her defenses and it might slip out, unbidden.

Marian sighed, taking a sip of her water. The wine looked nice. Like, *really nice.* She squinted as she studied the label. What sort of language was that? Foreign symbols crawled across the label, a strange language. She picked the bottle up, studying the origin information. *Minarak, Parsabad.*

Her eyes widened. No fucking way. What sort of weirdness was that? She set the bottle down and looked around again, as if Omar might materialize. A pipe dream if she'd ever had one.

She dragged her fingertips over the white linen tablecloth, waiting for Layla to return, until a movement caught her eye. Something fluttered in the air. She looked up and gasped. It was a butterfly. A black and blue butterfly heading straight for her. Followed by another one…and another.

She furrowed a brow, trying to understand what the hell was going on. Why were there butterflies in here? She craned her neck to see someone, anyone, that might be able to explain this. Was this part of the restaurant's shtick, and she just didn't know about it? Maybe that's why Layla brought her here, for the butterflies. God, where was Layla?

Marian sipped her water and then choked, spraying water everywhere over the tablecloth. Omar was in the doorway. He was in the fucking doorway across the room, the same one Layla had disappeared through. Tears pricked her eyes, and she covered her mouth, struggling to make sense of it. Either Layla was secretly Omar…or Omar had flown across the ocean after her.

Her lip trembled under her palm as he approached, his dark eyes set on her. More butterflies fluttered in the air as he came near, framing him in the most ethereal way. Maybe this was just a dream, spawned from heartbreak and intense longing. That still seemed a legitimate possibility.

"Marian." Omar slid onto the banquette next to her, reaching for her hand. The warmth of him rooted her to her spot, and a few tears escaped.

"Why are you here?"

Omar smiled a little. "You left before I could make things right."

Another tear escaped. "So you came to me?"

He nodded, wiping away a tear with his rough thumb. "Marian, I love you."

Her whole body quaked with the admission, and she crumpled into his arms. He held her, gently rocking back and forth, as she cried.

"I'm sorry for how everything went down," he whispered. "I never used you. You were always right by my side. I made sure that everyone knows you had the most to do with that deal…and that I just signed it."

Marian shook a little, letting his words wash over her. The tears wouldn't stop coming, but his scent was a balm she hadn't counted on.

"I just want to be with you," he murmured, stroking her hair. "You're the only woman that makes me feel free again. I want to be free, with you at my side."

Marian clutched at the lapels of his jacket, the tears finally subsiding. She looked up at him, searching his face for clues that this was really happening. The contours of his jawline, nose, the shape of his eyes, were such a relief to look at again—even after just days apart—that it prompted more tears.

"Goddammit," she sputtered, resting her forehead against his chest. "I love you too. Where did you get these butterflies?"

His warm hand smoothed over her back. "My father has been involved with conservation societies for a very long time. And occasionally, they're released back into the wild."

Marian groaned. "Like you?"

Omar's body shook as he laughed. "Exactly."

Marian looked up at him again, her face feeling damp and messy. "You're a real keeper, you know that?"

"I try my best," he murmured, rubbing his thumb over her chin. And then he pressed his lips to hers, an electric kiss zipping through her, making her toes tingle. "I want to keep this for as long as I can," Omar murmured, sliding his hand around the back of her neck.

Marian sighed, slinging her arms around him. Thank God this was real, this was happening. Because there was nobody else she wanted to have at her side. "Oh yeah? Well how do you suggest we do that, when we live half a world apart?"

"There are ways." He nuzzled his face against hers. "I could always move to New York. Or you could come claim your new job in Parsabad as Negotiations Director."

She inhaled sharply. "You're kidding."

"I've talked to my father and Mr. Thomas." He smiled warmly as he ran his fingers through her hair. She could look up into his eyes for a lifetime and still want more of it. "They both agree the change would be great for the company. And a bigger challenge for you, since you proved yourself with the National Oil deal. If you're open to the idea."

Her mouth fell open, ideas springing to life. A move to Parsabad? Omar at her side? A new, more challenging role? Not a single doubt crept into her mind. She could only feel excitement, could only see hope.

"*Yes*," she blurted.

Omar chuckled, brushing his lips against hers. "Don't you want to think about it for a little bit first?"

"I've never felt anything more right in my life," she said, hooking her arms around his neck. "God, it just makes so much sense. All of it. Especially *you*."

"So you won't have a problem coming to be with me…for a very long time…" Omar's gaze turned boyish and shy. "Like maybe forever."

Marian couldn't fight the smile. She fingered the collar of his jacket, admiring the immaculate trim of his hairline. Forever had seemed like a possibility with him from the beginning, even when it made no sense. Now it was the only thing that made sense. "That sounds like a pretty good start to me."

END OF THE SHEIKH'S UNRULY LOVER

ALMASI SHEIKHS BOOK TWO

PLUS: Love your sexy Sheikhs? Keep reading for an exclusive excerpt from Leslie North's bestselling novel, Sharjah Sheikhs Book One, **The Sheikh's Forced Bride.**

THANK YOU!

Thank you so much for purchasing and reading my book. It's hard for me to put into words how much I appreciate my readers. If you enjoyed this book, please remember to leave a review. I want to keep you guys happy! I love hearing from you :)

For all books by Leslie North visit:

Her Website: LeslieNorthBooks.com

Facebook: fb.com/leslienorthbooks

Get SIX full-length novellas by *USA Today best-selling author* Leslie North for FREE! Over 548 pages of best-selling romance with a combined 1091 FIVE STAR REVIEWS! Sign-up to her mailing list and get your FREE books at: Leslienorthbooks.com/sign-up-for-free-books

Sneak Peek

THE SHEIKH'S *forced bride*

Blurb

Sheikh Khalid Al-Qasimi's playboy ways have finally caught up with him. After creating a scandal during a diplomatic visit to America, Khalid is given a choice by his father—marry or face banishment. Rather than lose his family, Khalid bows to his father's wishes but an outspoken American interrupts Khalid's would-be wedding. Now Khalid has a new plan that might please his father, secure his inheritance and leave Khalid still able to go on with his life …he'll take the beautiful American as his bride— and then his father will hate her so much he'll beg Khalid not to get married after all.

Journalist Casey Connolly has never been afraid to share her opinions. While researching an article on arranged marriages, she lands in trouble when she crashes a royal wedding to get a quote from the attending American guests.. The sexy groom offers to set her free if she'll step into the role of his fiancée—just for a short time. Seeing a chance to get the scoop she needs, Casey agrees.

Soon there's no denying the chemistry they share. But Casey's boss is pushing her to complete her piece and head back to the States, while Khalid's father is still pushing for a hasty wedding. Will this pseudo-romance become the real thing or buckle under all the pressure being put on these two?

Get your copy of The Sheikh's Forced Bride from

www.LeslieNorthBooks.com

Excerpt

Sheikh Khalid Al-Qasimi took a deep breath to steady his nerves and let it out. He stared at the enormous wood doors in front of him. Drawing another slow breath, he put his hands on the brass door handles. Once he stepped through those doors, his life would change forever. And not for the better.

Letting go of the door, he shook his arms out and looked down at his traditional white robes of his country.

From behind, Ahmed's deep voice carried to Khalid. "She makes a beautiful bride, and Mehmood is a very traditional man, so I'm sure your wedding night with your bride will be a memory to treasure." Ahmed stepped up and nudged his brother's arm.

Khalid shot him a scornful look. "You are partly to blame for our father making me do this. I'm not interested in Mehmood or his daughter. And I don't care if she's a virgin. Do you think the women we saw in America were virgins?"

Ahmed shrugged. "You knew this day was coming. Granted, maybe a day with father a bit less angry than he is just now."

"Wait until it's your turn. I suspect our father's mood has more to do with the level of our transgression and less to do with age. You're next, little brother." Khalid turned his attention to the door again, waiting for the peace he needed before walking through.

Ahmed shook his head and offered up a weak smile. "It was just one night of fun."

"Fun? A good time is one thing. Dishonor is another." Khalid placed a hand on his brother's shoulder. "And this is about family honor—and me keeping my place in our family. Now, go. I'll make my entrance behind you."

"If there were another way…" Ahmed let the words trail off.

Khalid had thought the same thing. But he knew his choices here—marry or lose everything. He was not ready to say goodbye to his brothers or to his homeland. So he would take the other option Father had put before him. He patted Ahmed's shoulder and dropped his hand.

Ahmed shook his head, pulled his black *bisht* with the gold trim over his shoulders and opened the doors. It was strange to see Ahmed in anything but the perfectly tailored suits he always wore. Ahmed stepped into the room, his white *keffiyeh* swaying as he walked.

Get your copy of The Sheikh's Forced Bride from

www.LeslieNorthBooks.com

Made in the USA
Middletown, DE
10 June 2020